Love and Vendetta

LOVE AND VENDETTA

VIOLA TEMPEST

Copyright

Copyright © 2022 by Viola Tempest

Website: www.violatempest.com

Cover design by Ann Fleur

Prologue

I*t was all so innocent...until it wasn't*

The year was 1940, and Halloween was usually a time of great terror for the citizens of Romania. With the myth of vampires running wild in Transylvania, many feared that death awaited them outside their homes, hiding behind closed doors and under sheets instead of celebrating with parties and endless sweets. Children weren't allowed to go outside, and neighborhood parents kept close together, hoping that the larger their crowd, the easier it'd be for them to ward off any abnormals.

However, not everyone in Romania lived under the constant worry of being eaten alive. Or at least, they didn't used to. Far off in the dark corners of Romania, sat a forbidden town torn by warfare and separation. The town of Marsonia was perched on the coast of the deadly Black Sea, where corpses floated and mercury poisoned. Marsonia used to be calm and prosperous, with its citizens living in peace and sharing their riches with each other; not a single calamity or argument was heard even from miles away.

Unfortunately, the town of Marsonia became ridden with misfortune when Queen Azra and her royal family traveled far from across the Baltic Sea, setting up camp in Marsonia to conquer as their own. Queen Azra and her people invaded Marsonia, crushing buildings and exterminating everyone who stood in their way. The citizens tried to stop her. Oh, how they tried so hard to prevent her from taking over their land, even putting up a fight to defend themselves.

But they weren't strong enough; they weren't prepared. Never before had they had to go into battle, so when one took them by surprise, they were no match. Not even close.

Queen Azra seized the entire eastern part of Marsonia to build her own empire, declaring herself the new ruler and intercepting all the goods and resources from merchants to claim what she wanted before throwing anything that remained at the citizens. Usually, there was nothing left.

Her empire, now called Luceria, was one of great stature and high status, from gold and platinum pillars and stairs to marble walls to a throne completely constructed from rubies and sapphires. She and her people ate well every night, with more food than any of them ever needed, incinerating many leftovers before sharing the rest with the west. People here lived prosperously, dressed like royalty and treated like kings and queens. They received the best medicine money could buy, education from the greatest scholars known, and they never had to worry about when they would get their next meal.

The west, however, known as Hibernia, wasn't so lucky. Hibernia was comprised of all the original residents of Marsonia. They watched in defeat as Queen Azra and her army burned down their homes, stole all their food and resources, and killed many of their friends and family. But there was nothing else they could do. They were powerless. Now, they were forced to live in closed corridors, hundreds of them piling up on top of one another due to the lack of space, and surviving on scraps, rats, and sadly, each other. They were also forced to live away from the sea, as the queen feared that they'd escape and tell the rest of the world what she was up to.

No, instead, they were forced to live in darkness, with nothing but damaged roads and ashes that used to be homes. There were no shops or hospitals in Hibernia, the people having to rely on what little generosity Azra showed them instead. At least one person in Hibernia would die every day, either from starvation or from murder.

On the last day of every month, the people of Hibernia had a chance, a chance to win more to eat than the mere scraps they were usually forced to live off of. On the last day of every month, Queen Azra would gather the men from every Hibernian family and send them off to survive or die. They called this Kismet. In this game of cat and mouse, the men of Hibernia were brought to the yard of the kingdom, where they were given exactly thirty seconds to run and evade the guards before they started going after them, gunning them down. Only the quickest would survive. Only the quickest would evade the piercing bullets. Thirteen minutes later, whoever remained from Hibernia brought back to the west a small basket of goods and medical supplies, more than they would've gotten over the course of an entire year.

However, this year, Vladimir Covici had decided to switch

things up, turning the game around and hunting down the upper class instead. No more than seven minutes into the chase, Vladimir grabbed onto the arm of one of the queen's men, forcing him to drop his rifle, before sinking his teeth straight into the guard's neck, draining him from his very essence until he was left with nothing but a shriveled and pale lifeless body.

The audience gasped at Vladimir's brute force of action, his pearly white fangs dripping with warm blood as he let the guard fall onto the grass. At first, the crowd was in shock, unsure of what their eyes were seeing. But then it registered.

"Demon!" One of the members of the upper class shouted while pointing to Vladimir.

Before Vladimir could even react, the entire crowd broke into a frenzy and began throwing pitchforks and torches at the man. He desperately tried to run, pushing bystanders aside and slashing at others to move out of his way, but there were simply too many of them. Soon enough, Vladimir Covici came crashing down as hundreds of guards lunged at him, tackling him to the ground and instantly killing him.

One

October 31, 1950

Marietta Covici watched in anticipation and nervousness as her mother fussed with her hair, turning her long locks into tightly neat braids.

She had been dreading this moment for the past several months, wishing that it was only a dream instead of the nightmare that she was currently living in.

Any second now, she'd be forced to wed the most ruthless man in all of town.

Oh, if only her father had been more careful! She could still hear her mother's words. The way she always told him to keep his fangs in his mouth and avoid revealing them to Luceria at all costs.

Never let the people see who you really are. Without hesitation, they will come after you and hunt you down until you are no more.

Marietta always thought it was nothing but a rumor, a tale told to children just to scare them, but it had proven to be the truth, a gruesome truth. And that was more than enough to make her want to hide away and never see the light of day again.

But no, her mother had other plans for her, plans she had no say in.

"You have to get ready to meet Lord Blackwell," she said as she combed through her hair.

Marietta was the most beautiful and desired woman in all of Hibernia, her beauty surpassing far beyond that of others, even more beautiful than the women of Luceria. And she didn't mind all the attention, all the glares the men gave her whenever they saw her. But knowing that she'd have to settle down and become someone's property was all beginning to get too much for her.

As her mother tried to gather another loose strand into a braid, Marietta took a step to the left.

"That's enough, Mother," she insisted.

Desdemona Covici released her daughter and closed the bedroom door.

"What you fear, my child, is the same thing I fear, but in order for you, in order for all of us, to remain safe from Queen Azra's people, you must do as I say and marry her eldest son. It's the only chance we have of surviving."

"Can't you protect me, Mom?" Marietta asked.

But Desdemona only shook her head. "You know I can't, darling. I'm not like you and your father. I'm not special. I'm just... human. I couldn't protect your father, and I can't protect you. I'm sorry."

With a sigh, Marietta took a seat. Her hands were sweaty, her mind all over the place.

"I don't want to go against any of your wishes," Marietta said. "I trust you, Mother."

Desdemona shook her head. Eyes placed on one of the pictures in the room. It was a picture of Marietta's father, and he was donning an elegant three-piece suit while holding his hat in front of him. He was smiling the way she always remembered.

It made Marietta uneasy to look at it, however. It had been over ten years since the incident, but she was still traumatized by his death. It was just so... so... unexpected. One minute, he was kissing her on the forehead and promising her he'd bring back a feast to die for, and the next, he was just gone, a motionless pile of flesh lying in the middle of Queen Azra's backyard.

In that picture, he looked so human, so similar to everyone else in town, which was why he had been able to get away with his hungry secret for so long.

If only he hadn't gotten so hungry, so ravenous for revenge and human blood. But he knew, they all knew, that animal blood could only get them so far, could only quell their hunger so much before they started craving more, an intensity so great that there was nothing strong enough to suppress it.

And because of that, the men who had already inflicted enough damage upon them finished him off and burnt him to ashes, coming after Desdemona and Marietta soon after. They charged through their front door, but before they could seize them and burn them too, Desdemona grabbed her daughter and what little they could grab, and rushed out the back door, abandoning their home full of memories of how happy they were just the day before.

After the murder of Vladimir, his wife and daughter went into hiding, camping out in the dark wilderness and spending every night in fear before they ran into Morgana Hastings, Desdemona's childhood friend.

"Morgana?" Desdemona asked.

"Desdemona? Is that really you?" Morgana asked in return.

Desdemona formed a smile across her face. "My goodness, everyone thought you'd died. No one has seen you in decades!"

Morgana nodded. "Yes, my dear Desdemona. My parents and I have been living in these woods for the past thirty years. We wanted a peaceful life, nothing too loud or chaotic. But then, Queen Azra and her men came. My parents went over by the Black Sea to fish, but they couldn't make it back in time, not before Queen Azra blockaded Marsonia and... and..." Her voice cracked.

Desdemona pulled her friend into a hug. "It's okay, Morgana. It's okay. Just let it out."

"She killed them! She bloody killed them!" Morgana broke out into tears, crying on Desdemona's thick shoulder. "I told them not to go. I told them we were fine. But they wouldn't listen. They assured me they'd make it back in time. Such fools."

"I'm sorry, Morgana."

"Desdemona, dear. Will you please stay with me? The days have been absolutely dreadful living all alone. And I'm too afraid to venture out into the rest of Hibernia. I know what happens out there."

Desdemona smiled again. "Actually...I'm glad we found

you." She ushered little Marietta out from behind her. "Say hello to Morgana, Marietta."

Shyly, Marietta gave a small wave. "Hi."

"We need a place to hide. Queen Azra's guards are after us, and we are in great need of help. My husband, Vladimir... was killed." Desdemona finished, bowing her head in sadness.

"What happened?" Morgana asked.

"Let's... let's just say he died in Kismet."

Morgana nodded in understanding. Although she didn't know the full story, and Desdemona couldn't drum up the nerve to tell her, Morgana didn't press for more and allowed them to stay in her cabin.

Her mother cried, her mind returning to the present. "Lord Blackwell is our last hope," she said to her daughter. "He is of high power, the treasured elder son of Queen Azra. If anyone can convince the queen to spare our lives, it's him. He still wants you, despite knowing who we are, who you are. You must take advantage of this. We have no choice. You must marry him."

"Yes, Mother," Marietta obeyed, feeling all the venom and anger seep away from her.

Despite her feelings of hate and disgust toward the man who was ten years her senior, she knew she had to follow her mother's wishes. After all, she only wanted what was best for her. Her father had sacrificed his life for them when he tried to retaliate. To fall victim also and let all that go to waste would be a disaster worse than any other.

Her father was gone. She had to be strong for her mother and keep them all safe. It no longer became a question of if, but when, she would have to make her way over to Castle Vesunna to meet her future husband. Sure, she contemplated running away, but with the guards out looking for her, she knew she wouldn't be able to get very far.

Sighing heavily again, she went downstairs, where Morgana was standing by the doorway with a suitcase in one hand. Although they'd only be there for a couple hours, after the incident with her father, Marietta knew she had to prepare herself for anything that may come her way.

Two

Whatever rumors were heard of Castle Vesunna didn't do it justice. It was more ominous than the rumors had said, rumors that included stories of people walking through those doors and never coming out.

Marietta gathered the folds of her skirt and dusted off her dress to shake the smell of horses and stable from her body. Part of her still hoped that the Lord of Castle Vesunna wasn't actually as ruthless as the tales she had heard. With her luck, maybe he'd be as handsome as his castle was.

The view from afar was nothing compared to the lavish hallways and sparkling chandeliers Marietta came face-to-face with as she entered the building, her dainty feet grazing along the silk red rug beneath her.

Morgana followed her, looking displeased. Pursing her thin lips, she looked with distrust at the guards, who were all standing still with their swords, eyes unmoving. Ever since they took her parents away from her, she'd wanted nothing but revenge, but she was smart enough to know that even one wrong move would be deadly for her.

Marietta chuckled at the silliness of the guards. Strong enough to take down a full-grown vampire but not strong enough to disobey even the slightest order from the queen. She waved a hand in front of one of the guards, trying to see if he'd blink. He didn't.

Morgana threw Marietta a look that would put Desdemona to shame. After all these years, the two of them behaved more and more similarly.

Lowering her gaze to hide her amusement, Marietta felt Morgana's eyes pass over her and then back again at the men.

"This isn't the time to be laughing," she said. "This is your future we're walking into. And ours. If you even blink weird and mess this all up, everything we had planned for is ruined."

However, Marietta had a different motive in mind. She didn't see this as walking into her future. No, she saw this as walking into her death, her life forever over as a free creature and forever bound as a slave once she uttered those two short words.

He was dark, they said. The Lord of Castle Vesunna, his moods ridden with sudden outbursts, and his orders of death to those who betrayed him; he was truly a ruthless leader. Sure, she feared him, just like she also feared the wave of anger and rage that she needed to protect her family from, a personality even the toughest of men didn't dare to go near.

Morgana cleared her throat while Marietta wiped away a single tear as they stood in front of the ornate wooden door. They didn't wait long before hearing a loud voice ordering the guards on the other side to move. The door soon swung open, and a man dressed in a long coat approached them, his brows low and his smile hypnotizing. Marietta felt her heart beat as she took a closer look at him. He was gorgeous, with his dark eyes and luscious hair. His natural beauty glistened under the light, enough to make her body swoon when he smiled at her.

"Ladies," he said, clearing his throat. His eyes passed between the two of them. "You are here to meet Lord Blackwell, I presume."

He said it as an omen rather than a big announcement. Marietta tried not to look too much into what that meant. She smiled her most seductive smile and lowered her gaze the way her mother had taught her to do.

"Yes, Lord..."

"Cross."

"Lord Cross," she said, smiling.

Marietta wondered if Lord Blackwell was as much of a gentleman or as handsome as Lord Cross was. It would be too good to be true, but she could still dream.

As Lord Cross guided them through the home, Marietta couldn't help but gaze around the room; the hallways were decorated with red roses and white lilies, and on every wall, hung a portrait of a relative from generation to generation, the faces of regal and nobility.

Soon, I will be the lady of the house, she thought.

Mere minutes later, she and Morgana found themselves facing another ornate door, guarded heavily by a similar army of guards.

"Halt!" said one of them. "Who are these filthy peasants, and what business do they have being here?"

Before Marietta could open her mouth to introduce

herself, her face turning pale, Lord Cross stepped up from behind them.

"Step aside, Winston. They're here for Blackwell."

With that, Winston shakily pointed toward the far west of the hallway, his fingers trembling as if filled with terror. The path down the hall was dark, lit with nothing but a small candle, with a red velvet rug that led them into a separate room.

Before Marietta's eyes could reach the light, she heard Morgana gasp.

At the other end of the hall lied a half-naked man, shirt ripped open, flushed skin in clear view.

Lord Blackwell.

"Huh? What? Who dares enter my chamber?" The man sprung up from his chair in agitation.

"Blackwell, this is Marietta, your...," Cross started to speak before he was rudely interrupted.

"Get out! Get out, now!"

Startled, Lord Cross turned back toward the girls and ushered them out of the room.

"We'll come back later," he apologized. "It seems that Lord Blackwell is feeling unwell."

As Marietta walked out, she couldn't shake the sensation that she was being watched. She began to realize that Blackwell was nothing like Cross, complete opposites really, and that made her begin to worry. Maybe she *was* making a huge mistake after all.

"Do you think the rumors about Blackwell are true? That he's really a...," Marietta turned to Morgana and began to ask.

"Silence!" Morgana hissed. "Lord Blackwell is an honorable and noble man. Don't you even dare let him hear such nonsense come out of your mouth. You're in the home of royalty. Learn your place."

Marietta quickly fell silent. Morgana was every bit like her mother. Even with pure rage rushing through her blood from what the royal family did to her, she still remained respectful. Everything she did was a copy of her mother. Guess it's true what they say, that when you've lived with someone long enough, you begin to act like them. Because of that, Marietta knew she had to trust that Morgana had nothing but her best interest in mind.

Marietta felt her stomach begin to churn, not because the thought of Blackwell repulsed her, but because she hadn't eaten for days. The feast of animals her mother served her wasn't nearly enough to quell her cravings, and she found herself salivating for something else. Someone else. But she couldn't. No, not after her father's murder. If she lost control now, she'd surely be killed. No, she had to be discreet, sneak it when she was sure no one was looking. No one could find out who they were, especially not Blackwell.

But then another vomit-inducing thought made her wrench, that she would soon become the wife of a drunk... and she had to simply accept that. Wealth, protection, and alcohol. That would become her new life.

She continued mulling over her thoughts when a tall figure came into sight. It was getting dark, and Marietta couldn't make out who the figure approaching her was, but suddenly, it came into her vision. It was Lord Blackwell.

He looked much better... and cleaner now that he wasn't covered in bottles and filth. His hair had been brushed, shirt buttoned, and his beard neatly trimmed. However, Marietta found herself more attracted to Lord Cross, the way he'd look at her with his striking eyes and dark black curls. Lord Blackwell, on the other hand, was already beginning to gray, with much shaggier hair and a less structured face. Plus, their personalities were as different as night and day.

"Marietta Covici," he grinned, looking at her.

A guard escorted Morgana away while Marietta was left

alone with Blackwell. She greeted him nervously as she curtsied and could smell the stench still lingering on his breath as he leaned in closer.

"I'd like to show you how things are done around here, in my home."

He grabbed her by the wrist. There was absolutely nothing tender or gentle about the way he did it. She tried to pull away, but he kept her in place.

"As my future wife, you must learn to do things my way. A lowly peasant like you can never disagree with anything I say. One step out of bounds, and you're done for. Do you understand me?" he demanded.

Sweat poured down her face as she fearfully nodded her head, silent. She didn't know how to respond to him, not only because she was at a loss for words, but because she feared that any response at all could set him off like a dynamite. Such evil words spewing from his mouth only made Marietta hate him that much more.

She gritted her teeth, thinking of all the ways she could get rid of him. The thought of marrying him made her sick to her stomach. She didn't care how much was at stake anymore.

Suddenly, she felt a hand reach up her backside, groping her in places she had never been touched before. Without hesitation, she reached a hand of her own out and slapped him hard across the face.

Her hand left a sizable mark on his cheek, but he only responded with a sinister grin.

"Feisty, are we? You're the first woman to have ever done this. Are you not afraid for your life if you disrespect a Lord? We'll have to work on fixing your attitude if you're to be my wife."

"No!" Marietta yelled. "I refuse to be your wife. I won't marry you."

But Blackwell could only laugh before reaching out his

hand again and grasping it around her neck, leaving Marietta to flail for oxygen while dangling in the air.

"We'll just see about that." He snarled before letting her fall to the ground.

He shook his head, dusted off his coat as if he'd been the one to grace the ground, and walked away.

Still lying on the ground, Marietta gasped for air. Her body was shaking, and angry tears formed from her eyes. She had never been so terrified of a human.

But she was strong, and she wasn't about to take this abuse lying down. The anger soon gave way to the desire for revenge, to take down Blackwell for his ruthless behavior, and teach him a lesson.

When she finally stood up, she found herself staring into the beautiful eyes of Lord Cross.

Why couldn't he have been the one I'm supposed to marry? He's everything I could ever ask for. Instead, I got stuck with a nightmare.

He placed a hand on her shoulder as she wiped off her tears with a sleeve. "I saw what Blackwell did to you. I wish I could tell you that he's not usually like that, but then I'd be lying." He took a deep breath. "I've known him since we were just mere kids, and he's had it far too easy in his life, spoiled by all the riches and wealth he could ever have. Now, he simply takes everything for granted. In a way, we can't really blame him. He doesn't know any better."

"What am I supposed to do? He's a tyrant! I can't vow to marry someone who has no problem locking me up whenever he chooses! I'm powerless."

At that, Lord Cross leaned in closer and whispered in her ear. "You didn't hear this from me, but see that man over there?"

He gestured toward a frail-shaped man with red hair and a red beard who stood by the gates with his arms crossed over his chest. "That's Nicolo. Of all the men in this castle, he's the only one I trust. Next time you meet with Blackwell, pretend to fall ill, and Nicolo will take you home on one of our stable horses. Grab your family, and go into hiding. And when you do, don't come out, no matter what anyone says. It won't take long for someone to realize what's happened and come find you. And let us never speak of this again," he finished before quickly scurrying away.

Three

That night, Desdemona received her daughter with open arms. As soon as Nicolo departed, Marietta ran upstairs to her room and drew herself a bath to wash the filth of Blackwell off from her body. She scrubbed against her skin so hard that the soap almost disintegrated on her fingers. She still had her plan in mind, but she'd need to speak to her mother first.

She dried herself off and changed into a nightgown before heading back downstairs. The familiar scent of home helped calm her down. She knew she'd need it when she broke the bad news to her mother.

"Mother," Marietta whispered, nodding her head in respect.

"So formal... You're only like this when you have bad news," Desdemona said, looking at her with a curious glance. "Tell me, is he as much of a monster as people say he is?"

The word *monster* escaped her lips with ridicule as she watched Marietta. A familiar sense of dread took root in Marietta's stomach.

"I know you, my dear. Even now as an adult, you're still as transparent to me as ever," she continued, walking across the room closer to her daughter.

"Yes," Marietta could only whisper. "He's worse than a monster. I don't want to marry him anymore." Her eyes began to water, and her cheeks turned red when Desdemona glided her fingers across Marietta's neck.

"I see he has left a mark on you. A mark of passion, perhaps?"

But Marietta shook her head. Sometimes, she longed for the woman her mother used to be before her father's death, the woman who showed her affection and comfort rather than disdain and disappointment, constantly looking out for her own survival rather than Marietta's happiness.

"Well, what's your solution then? Without Lord Blackwell, we're as good as dead," Desdemona demanded.

"I... I don't know, okay? All I know is I can't go back there. He hurts me, insults me, and he's always drinking. I never want to go back to that disgusting man."

"I'm sorry, dear. But you're an adult now, and sometimes, adults need to do things they don't want to if it means benefiting everyone else. With your father gone, we need this, no matter how hard it might be. I'm afraid you have no choice but to go back to Castle Vesunna and wed Lord Blackwell."

Desdemona gave her daughter a kiss on the forehead before retreating to her room.

But Marietta refused to accept defeat. Her mother didn't know the pain that she would have to face, and if she didn't want to help her, she'd have to take matters into her own hands. She remembered the way Lord Cross looked at her and felt the rush of euphoria spread through her body.

The words spilled out abruptly as if on a schedule, "I have to kill Lord Blackwell," she whispered to herself, clenching hard on her fists.

She was nervous about her plan, so nervous that she shattered a vase into pieces.

"What's the matter?" Morgana asked. "You look like you're ready to pass out."

Marietta knew she couldn't risk exposing her plan to Morgana. The first thing she'd do is run to tattle on her.

"Nothing," she responded instead and knelt down to pick up the broken shards.

"Now is not the time to start being clumsy, Marietta. You need to show the Lord that you're a capable young woman who can take care of him and his future children."

Not a chance in hell, Marietta thought.

She could almost picture it. Her mother and Morgana lying in riches while she was trapped in a dungeon bearing loud and needy children she couldn't even stand. She'd have to feed that drunk a hearty breakfast every morning, right before he would strike her with his fist for the food being lukewarm.

Sure, everyone else would be happy, at her expense. She was only eighteen, and she refused to slave away her life just for a false illusion of safety.

"Your mother's happy, you know. She talks all the time about how you'll finally have a man to take care of you after your father died," Morgana continued.

But at what cost? Everyone's happy, but at what cost?

The image of Blackwell conjuring in Marietta's mind made her lose her lunch, bolting up the stairs and emptying a mouth full of bile into a bucket beside her bed. Even thirty miles was not a great enough distance to separate Marietta from that vile man.

"And what if I refuse to marry him?" she turned to ask Morgana as she ran up to check in on her.

"Death, my child. Death by a hundred swords will befall upon our family if you walk away from this now."

THE NEXT MORNING, MARIETTA WALKED OUT INTO the town of Hibernia, contemplating about the difficult choice she had to make. Her hometown was already in ruins, with no resources to live off of, and nothing to live for other than to hope that Queen Azra pitied them enough to share her fortune. She looked around. People were sleeping on the streets, wearing torn rags, and covered in dirt. She'd be surprised if she could even find one person who wasn't infected by some sort of bacterial illness.

She walked a little further, down to where her favorite bakery used to be. Her mother would take her every Sunday morning to get her favorite treat, a vanilla frosted Papanași. She could still taste the sugary cheese-filled doughnut lifting up her mood, the warmth of the treat giving her a feeling of comfort and security.

"Eat up, sweetie." Her mother would say. "We can always get another one if you want."

Young Marietta shook her head. "No thanks, Mother. I'm full for now. I'm sure there's plenty more where this came from."

Now, it was nothing but a pile of rotten wood and ash.

She wished she had never uttered those words, those

words she would blame herself for saying and jinxing her town. Sometimes, she'd sit in her room alone and wonder whether everything that had happened to Marsonia would've turned out differently if only she had done things differently in her own life. Maybe she should've taken that second Papanaşi. Maybe her mother should've eaten one, too. Maybe she could've been more understanding whenever her father tried to train her to control her hunger pangs. Maybe now, she wouldn't feel like she was starving.

She continued walking down the dilapidated road, the road that used to be filled with happy citizens and visitors dancing to the sound of music, with a beer in one hand and a partner in the other. Bands from all over the country would gather together and strum their instruments, and restaurants would hand out free meals to join in with the celebration. The soft pretzel stand to her right used to have a long line of hungry folks waiting, and the ice cream shop to her left used to see hundreds of laughing kids a day. She looked at them now, barely recognizable. She couldn't even tell anymore where one building ended and another one started.

She allowed her steps to take her to wherever her feet wanted to go. With no plan or hope left in her mind, her only wish was that no one would shoot her. Desdemona had always warned her not to go outside, where there was a high chance someone would recognize who she was and kill her on the spot. And Marietta had heard the words "witch," "demon," and "monster" thrown at her father so many times that she should be scared. But she wasn't. It just seemed like death wasn't nearly as terrifying as the thought of being the next Lady Blackwell.

Eventually, she found herself face-to-face with the wall, the notorious wall that separated Hibernia and Luceria. It was massive, too tall for anyone to climb over, and too long for anyone to try and sneak around it. And even if they could, even if they tried to squeeze themselves in between the metal bars of the frame, the barbed wire and electrified fence would surely stop them. Nonetheless, the massive wall was impossible to break through. The only people who could were the high guards of Luceria who all possessed the key for the bulletproof metal door that connected the two lands.

Marietta scoffed. It wasn't like she was all that interested in going to the other side anyway.

"Marietta?" She heard a voice call out to her.

She spun her head around behind her, unsure of where the voice was coming from. Part of her began to shiver, her fingers crossed that her last moment on Earth wouldn't be staring at the Wall of Separation that had ruined her life.

"Marietta, over here!" The voice called out again.

This time, she peered through the fence and saw Lord Cross, even more radiant in the bright daylight than he had been when she first saw him. She walked a little closer, unsure of what he wanted. She almost wanted to reach out and touch him, but that decision would be fatal.

"Lord Cross, it's a pleasure to see you again." Marietta curtsied.

"What are you doing out in broad daylight? I thought I warned you to grab your family and go into hiding." His voice grew louder as he stepped closer toward her. "You're going to get both of us killed if Blackwell finds out that you're not actually ill."

I... I... I couldn't...," Marietta stuttered. "I just couldn't live with myself knowing that I'd let the fear of one man dictate how I lived my life. I don't deserve that, Lord Cross. I just don't!"

She expected him to become angry, to run inside the castle and tell the guards to seize her for Lord Blackwell. But he didn't. Instead, he just smiled.

"I understand that. Same with my mother, Queen Azra.

That's why Blackwell is her favorite, and I'm the illegitimate child she never wanted. We can't win them all, I guess."

Marietta smiled. Lord Cross *definitely* wasn't the tyrant that his brother was, and his words made her feel closer to him.

"Anyway," Cross continued. "Since you are here, how are you feeling? I see the mark Blackwell left hasn't yet gone away."

"No," Marietta whispered.

She pulled a hand up to her neck and touched the mark left behind, imprinted like a scar onto her skin.

A saddened look graced Cross' face. "I know my brother isn't exactly a gentleman—"

"Gentleman?!" Marietta nearly shouted. "He's... He's a monster!"

"That's mainly when he drinks, though. Usually, he's still pretty erratic, but nowhere near as psychotic."

But Marietta could only scoff in disbelief. "I find that incredibly difficult to believe, given the rumors all over town about how he has no soul. Why are you defending a monster?"

"Well, he *is* my brother, after all. And I'm not defending him, exactly. I just understand how he'd gotten this way. His entire life, our mother spoiled him, gave him the life she wanted for herself, along with the mentality of getting it. It's not completely his fault he became like this. He doesn't know any better."

"But why me?" Tears began to pour from Marietta's eyes. "Out of all the women in the town of Marsonia, why'd he have to pick me? I'm nothing but a lowly, filthy peasant. He could've had any one of the high-class damsels. Why'd he have to choose me?"

Cross blushed, rubbing the back of his neck. "Well, Marietta, I'm sure this isn't news to you, but you're the prettiest one, more beautiful than even the women of Luceria. It isn't much of a surprise that Blackwell would choose you."

"Pretty? You think I'm pretty?" Marietta asked. This time, it was her turn to blush.

Cross nodded. "Yeah, everyone does. To be honest, I was a little jealous when I found out that my brother was marrying you. Sure, he always got his way, but this one really stung."

"Lord Cross?" Marietta asked.

"Please, Marietta, call me Cross. No need to be formal."

"Cross," she corrected herself. "I have a confession."

Cross raised a brow, unsure of what she meant.

"I have a confession," Marietta repeated. "When I went to Castle Vesunna, it was you I had my eyes on, not Lord Blackwell."

Cross widened his eyes, almost in disbelief. "Me?" he barely whispered.

Marietta nodded before looking away. She wasn't sure how Cross would react to her confession, or whether he'd turn her in to his brother. She winced and turned around, expecting the worst, when Cross walked straight through the Wall of Separation and into Hibernia.

He placed a hand on her shoulder, and when she turned back to face him, he was smiling.

"What? How did you—" she asked, confused.

"Get across the wall? I'm royalty, remember? Anything I say goes. Plus, it definitely helps that I swiped the key from Nicolo when he wasn't looking."

Marietta chuckled. "What are you doing here, anyway? No one from Luceria ever comes into Hibernia. They all think it's too below them."

"True, most of the upper class do think like that. But I'm not like that. I never agreed with what my mother did to your town, and if I had any say at all, I would've stopped her, but it's either follow along or die. Not really much of a choice there." He reached down and grabbed her hands in his and kissed them.

"What are you doing?" she asked.

He shrugged. "Honestly, I don't know. And I know I shouldn't be saying this. If anyone ever found out, it's off with my head. But I don't think you should be marrying Blackwell. I know you're the chosen one, and therefore, you're expected to, but your heart is so pure. I can sense it. I think it'll be wasted on someone like him."

"What are you suggesting?"

"Me, Marietta. Be with me instead."

Flushed, Marietta didn't know what to say. It's what she'd wanted; the beautiful Lord Cross wanted her just as much as she wanted him. She had dreamt about this moment since she first saw him, but now that it was happening, she couldn't find the right words to say. Instead, she pulled her hands away from his and ran away.

When she finally arrived back at Morgana's cabin, she was out of breath. The living room was empty as Marietta took off her shoes and ran a few fingers through her hair.

"And where were you?" Desdemona asked.

Marietta jumped. She wasn't expecting anyone to be downstairs. Her mother usually spent half the day in bed, still grieving about the loss of Vladimir, and Morgana usually went out back during this time of day to chop down more firewood.

"I... um... just went for a walk," Marietta answered quietly.

"A walk? Where?"

Marietta remained quiet. She wasn't allowed to step out of the woods, ever, and if her mother found out that she went into town, she'd have a heart attack. Hell, if she ever found out that her daughter went to the wall, the deadly wall where anyone who looked even the slightest suspicious was killed on the spot, she'd wouldn't just have a heart attack, she'd pull out a knife and murder her own kin.

"I said, where?!" Desdemona asked again, the vein on her temple looking like it's ready to explode, when Marietta didn't answer.

"Just... just around," she whispered.

Her mother crossed her arms over her chest. With a snide grin, she said, "I don't believe you. You're lying."

"I'm not, I swear!"

"You're lying! If your father were still here—"

Marietta burst into tears. "Well, he's not, okay? He's dead! And it's all your fault for letting him go to the castle!" She ran up to her room and slammed the door shut. She knew she was acting unfair to her mother. She knew it wasn't her fault that her father died, but she just couldn't help but resent her for forcing her to marry Lord Blackwell against her own will.

LATER THAT NIGHT, WHILE MARIETTA SAT QUIETLY in her dark room contemplating about the life she was about to lose when she had barely even gotten a chance to live it yet, she heard a knock on her window. Well, it was more of a thud than a knock, but it was loud enough to catch her attention. She stood up and looked out the slightly cracked pane, seeing none other than Lord Cross himself standing by her front door.

Shocked, Marietta threw her nightgown on over her slip and slowly walked down the wooden stairs, careful as to not make any noise that would wake up her mother and Morgana. She creaked open the front door and stepped outside, curtsying as she saw Lord Cross.

"What are you do—I mean, Lord Cross, your majesty, how may I be of assistance?" Her heart was pounding as she spoke. Sure, she was glad to see him, but she didn't know why he was here.

Had he found out what I really am? Had he come to capture and kill me, like his family did to my father?

Her body was shaking, trembling beneath her nightgown as she slowly looked up to make eye contact with Cross. To her surprise, he was grinning at her.

"What did I say about calling me that?"

"Sorry."

He laughed. "Don't sweat it."

"But what *are* you doing here, really?" Marietta asked again. "Have you come to capture me and bring me back to Lord Blackwell?" She gestured toward his horse.

"The complete opposite, actually. I came to ask you to run off with me. So, we can be together. I can get you out of here, out of this diseased town where someone as beautiful as you clearly doesn't belong."

"I... I don't understand," Marietta asked, confused.

"Don't marry Blackwell. Be with me, and together, we can travel the world, see all the great wonders, and be happy, with each other. I see the pain you have in your heart, Marietta, and it saddens me. Run off with me, Marietta. We can leave tonight."

"But what about my mother and Desdemona? I can't just leave them here. What about Lord Blackwell? Once he finds out that I'm gone, he's going to come looking for me."

Cross' face dropped. It was as if Marietta had just torn out his heart and soul and crushed them. "I guess you're right. I got a little ahead of myself. This wouldn't work. Not with Blackwell in the picture. This wouldn't work at all. How could I have been such a fool?!" He gave her a hug and turned away. "I guess this was a dumb idea. I'm sorry for ruining your night."

He slowly walked back to his horse, when Marietta ran after him and grabbed his arm.

"Cross, wait!" She leaned up and kissed him on the lips, locking her arms around his neck.

She felt him pulling her closer, his hands on her waist, and he kissed her back.

"Wow, not that I'm complaining, but where did that come from?" Cross asked when they finally pulled away.

"You're right, Cross. Let's run away together. Get out of this shit town and travel the world. Together. You and me."

"But what about Blackwell?"

Marietta shook her head. "Don't worry about him. Let me handle it. I'll make sure he doesn't come after us. Everything will be fine. Just fine."

Later that night, Marietta tasted blood in her mouth, sweet warm blood of a human being that she hadn't gotten the chance to experience for years. Waiting until her mother and Morgana fell asleep, she snuck out and made her way to Castle Vesunna.

Sure, she wouldn't have been able to cross the wall, not as herself anyway. Walking up to the guards, she pretended to be an elderly woman in need, hoping the guards' empathy was enough to fall for her plan. It worked. Upon falling over onto the ground, the guards opened the gate to help her up.

Stupid fools, she thought. *Hasn't Azra taught you any better than to open the gate for a Hibernian?*

In one swift motion, Marietta grabbed one of the guards by the neck and sunk her teeth into his thick, pale skin, draining him of his essence in the form of warm, delicious blood, while holding down the other guard with her knee.

"Don't worry, honey. You're next." She sneered at the man

on the ground, then went back to the man beside her, slurping until he was completely dry.

She felt powerful. For the first time since her father was killed, she felt like she was avenging his death. All those years trapped, filled with anger that she couldn't do anything, finally caught up to her, and she found herself struggling to stop.

"Die, you imbecile, die. I hope it's a painful death," she whispered into the ear of the second guard before piercing her fangs straight into his flesh as well.

When she finally finished off guard number two, she eased her way across the wall into Luceria. Sure, she had been in Luceria before, the tragic day when she was forced to find out that her future husband was nothing but a complete asshole, but she was brought directly to Castle Vesunna that day; she never had the chance to see the rest of the town. And though it was dark, the town of Luceria was much more beautiful than she'd ever imagined, a complete contrast from Hibernia.

The buildings and homes were twinkling bright, with the fresh smell of oxygen releasing from the lush trees as opposed to the stench of garbage and rotting flesh back home. The roads were paved, clean, and even with the horses and carriages lining the streets, the smell in the air was still magnificent, the fragrant ocean breeze reminding her of when she was just a toddler, and her father would bring her by the pier and stare out into the vast ocean, dreaming of so many possibilities life would bring her. But that was all gone now, with all hope lost. Even if she wanted to sit by the pier, even if she wanted to bring back the memories of her father and her childhood, the dock was now guarded by an entire army. One step onto it, and Marietta would be shot and burned on the spot, just like Vladimir.

Luceria was a quiet town, with no stragglers on the streets after nine, and everyone had a home they belonged in, a right rather than a luxury like it was back home in Hibernia. However, silence also made it much harder for her to not get caught. Once the two guards by the wall were found, there would be a massive search party looking for her. Oh, she could still remember the darkness and emptiness in her father's eyes when they burned him, the flesh melting off his skin as the crowd threw rocks at him and called him a demon spawn. She couldn't live that same fate. She just couldn't. Her mother and Morgana would be left powerless to defend themselves.

No, she had to remain discreet, make her way to Castle Vesunna without anyone noticing her. One positive about being a half-vampire was that her steps remained incredibly light, almost as if she was floating in air.

It didn't take an expert to realize when she was close to the castle. Out in the yard, the guards were burning slaves for amusement, making them dance for a chance at some morsels of bread while the guards laughed and threw crumbs at them. The slaves were almost always Hibernians, those who have tried to climb across the wall but were caught instead. They remained in the cells of the castle. The others, however few, were Lucerians. Despite claiming to care for her own people, Queen Azra was ruthless to those who broke the law, treating even her own kind as worthless prisoners when they stepped out of bounds. Immunity didn't exist in Luceria, not even for her own family.

When she finally arrived at Vesunna, she eased her way up the main tower and toward Lord Blackwell's corridor, the rage and hunger of an angry beast looming inside her. Luckily, no one saw her as she climbed through the window, with only the dark night and howling wolves around to notice what she was up to. As she closed in, all she could smell was the stench of alcohol and cigars coming in waves from the northern direction of the castle.

Her senses were always better at night. When everybody

else was asleep, she'd usually sneak out and explore her freedom in the deep forest behind her home, ravaging through hordes of whatever animal she could find.

As she inched closer, she could almost taste him. Her mouth salivating with hunger and desire, paired with her lust for revenge, left almost no chance for her to stop. She felt absolutely no love for the man, only pure, righteous anger.

"You'll soon feel what it's like to have a taste of your own medicine," she whispered, licking her lips.

However, as she inched closer toward the man in slumber, her jacket caught onto a nail sticking out from one of the chairs, and she fell over.

"Marietta?" Blackwell asked tiredly as he turned on the light. Then he quickly sat up and back up against his bedframe when he finally realized what he was seeing. "What are you doing here?! I thought you were sick. I thought you had fallen ill and had to go home." Then he squinted his eyes. "You were never really sick to begin with, were you?"

Marietta tried to keep herself from getting sick. The stench of liquor was still potent in his room, as if he'd over-dosed himself with alcohol even in his sleep. She couldn't stand to look at him, the sneer on his face so similar to a monster that she couldn't care less if he died at her hands or not. She just wanted him gone. She knew she had remained silent for far too long, that if she didn't say anything soon, he'd begin to suspect what she was up to. She could lie, perhaps. Tell him that she made a mistake and came to surprise him, profess her love to him. And he may possibly fall for it, if she were charming enough, but the bile that kept threatening to rise from her throat made her reconsider.

And before she had a chance to come up with another answer, he jumped out of bed and straight toward her, his hand wrapped around her neck once again, in the same spot it had been just mere days ago.

"I said, you were never really sick to begin with, were you?!" Lord Blackwell shouted even louder.

His face was fuming red, and if Marietta didn't know better, she could've sworn she saw smoke steaming out from his ears. A flash of déjà vu overcame her senses, and she felt her body trembling at his touch, fearing for her life that he would end up murdering her.

"I... I... I was, my Lord. I *had* fallen quite ill, but my mother was able to gather some fresh herbs from the wilderness, and now I feel much better. I came back to see you. To tell you that I'm alright. I miss you, my Lord. You are my future husband, and I wanted you to know that I'm fine." She didn't know what she was saying, but the rush of adrenaline caused the words to spill out of her in attempts to save her own life. She expected Blackwell to call her out on her bullshit, to throw her across the room for continuing to lie to him, but he didn't. Instead, he smiled and released her, his pity for her weakening him.

But the same couldn't be said for Marietta. As soon as he released her and retreated to his bed, calling out for her to join him, she quickly rushed over and seized his neck with her own hands, her grip tightening as the air escaped from him. He didn't move an inch; the initial shock paralyzing him. She could only imagine what was going through his head at that moment. The shy peasant girl he thought could barely chop her own wood, now had the upper hand and was threatening his life right when he decided to let down his guard. A list of regrets was probably crossing his mind, and he couldn't even call for help. Her hand was gripped so perfectly around his trachea that one wrong move could prove fatal.

Instead, he could only look at her, his eyes pleading her to release him, but Marietta was smarter than that. She knew that as soon as she let go, Blackwell would seize her, call the guards, and she'd be burned at the stake.

She shook her head. No, she came all this way; there was no turning back now. She had to complete her mission. If she walked away now, she'd surely be captured for killing the two guards. It was pretty obvious who had done it since she was the only free Hibernian on this side of town.

She gripped her hands even tighter, paralyzing him even more. She then lowered her mouth down to the pulsating vein in his neck. It was only until she sunk her sharp fangs deep inside his pale neck did he rediscover his ability for movement. A scream tried to escape him, but he was already too far gone. All Marietta could taste were raw blood and fresh human meat, sucking and draining him of his soul. When she was through with him, blood poured from her lips, and she dropped him to the ground, lying there motionless and lifeless.

"Do I take you as my lawfully wedded husband, Lord Blackwell?" She spat his blood out on top of him. "Not a chance in hell."

Without feeling guilt or hesitation, she licked her lips clean, climbed out of the tower, and descended, failing to see the dark figure hiding out in the shadows as she made her way to Lord Cross.

Four

L ord Cross slowly climbed out of bed when he heard a faint knock on his window. It was three in the morning, and the expression on his face was evident that he needed his beauty sleep. Marietta never understood why mortals had this problem. She never grew tired, despite having a long day. Eventually, her days just all blended together.

When he saw Marietta standing outside his balcony, he quickly rushed over to let her in.

"Marietta, what are you doing here? And at this hour?

Quick, come in. It's freezing outside!" he whispered aggressively, helping her into his room before anyone else saw her.

He then looked down at his nightgown. His plain white cotton broadcloth turned his face red compared to Marietta's black leather jumpsuit. He quickly turned away and walked toward his closet to throw a velvet overcoat over himself before returning to Marietta.

"I came to see you, my Lor... I mean, Cross," she responded.

But the look on his face was still perplexed. "How did you even get past the guards? How'd you get across the wall, and all the way up my tower? I have so many questions." Then he raised a brow and leaned in closer to her before whispering, "Are you some sort of supernatural creature?"

Marietta gulped. Sweat dripped down the back of her neck. Although she knew he was probably joking, she couldn't help but feel incredibly nervous that she may have just been caught.

Does he know? She thought to herself. *No, he can't. He's just messing around.*

"I have my ways. I'm very, very smart, and a great climber. I live in a forest and have climbed trees my entire life. The towers of Castle Vesunna are no sweat." She lied instead.

"If my mother found out that you hacked her system, it's off with your head. You know that, right?"

"Of course, I do. That's why I came here to tell you that we should leave tonight. Let's get out of here. Ride far and away from this town. Together, you and me," she pleaded as she tugged against his arm.

But Lord Cross refused to budge so easily. He was still confused as to what her motives were for this impromptu visit. "But what about my brother? What would we even tell him?"

"Don't worry about it. I've taken care of it. He won't be bothering us, I promise." She continued to pull.

"What do you mean, he won't be bothering us? What exactly did you do?"

Putting on her mask again, Marietta took a deep breath before speaking. "Another reason why I came here tonight was to talk to Lord Blackwell. I told him that I didn't love him, and there was nothing he could do to make me love him. I convinced him that he'd much rather find a woman who could be loyal to him and serve him without any regrets than with someone who was repulsed by him." She sighed. Never in her life had she had to lie so much, and the feeling of knowing she could on the spot made her feel powerful.

Cross grimaced. "Is that so? Maybe I should go talk to him and see how he's do—"

"No!" Marietta nearly shouted, then slapped her hands over her mouth to muffle herself. "I mean, I did *just* tell him. I'm sure he's still pretty angry. I don't believe that's a good idea."

It took several more minutes of convincing, but soon, both Lord Cross and Marietta were sneaking out the back door of Castle Vesunna and loading up onto a stallion.

"I know just the place we can go while we figure out our next plan," Cross whispered while Marietta threw a cloak over her head to shield her appearance from the guards. "It's a little town not far from here called Valeria, a free town without rules or laws, a town where people were free to be whoever they wanted.

"Wait, before we leave, I need to say farewell to my mother and Desdemona. Can we please make a quick stop?"

Cross nodded and turned around in the opposite direction. When they came to the wall, he was surprised to find it open. "That's strange. Where are the guards?" he asked.

Marietta tensed up, afraid that her plan might have just been ruined because of her hunger.

"Hello?" Lord Cross called out. "Is anyone here?"

Luckily for Marietta, the moon had shifted, and it was now too dark for Cross to see the dead bodies still lying wilted on the ground.

With no answer, Cross conceded. "Hmm, we can't just leave the gate open like this. I'll call for reinforcement when we come back. Right now, we need to get you packed."

Marietta nodded, her heart relieved as the stallion leapt over the bodies of the guards.

MARIETTA VIGOROUSLY SCRUBBED AT HER SKIN when they arrived at her cabin. The noise must've woken up Desdemona, and she had on a look of horror when she found her daughter covered in blood. She had finally taken off her jacket, the jacket that hid the sight from Cross, and her arms were stained red with the blood of the guards and Blackwell.

After taking one look at her daughter and finding a piece of fabric dangling by the nail on the window, it didn't take long for Desdemona to figure out what she had done.

"Tell me you didn't," she demanded.

"I didn't what?" Marietta asked, playing innocent.

"Marietta Covici, you know you are supposed to only drink the blood of animals. Human blood is off limits. Tell me that isn't human blood stained on your teeth."

"Mother, you know I would never disrespect you like that. Of course, it's animal blood. Rabbit, to be precise. I was feeling a little woozy, so I snuck out for a little snack. It's all innocent, I promise."

After Marietta was finished scrubbing, Desdemona

followed her into her bedroom as Marietta started to pack her things.

"And where do you think you're going?" Desdemona asked with a stern tone.

"Castle Vesunna, Mother. To Lord Blackwell. Since I am to soon be his wife, he requested my presence there with him."

Her mother knew her well, and Marietta was sure that she could see right through her lie, but instead, Desdemona wrapped her arms around her daughter and squeezed her into a hug.

"I knew you would come around to your senses! I knew you would change your mind and realize how important it is for all of us that you wed Lord Blackwell."

Marietta felt a sharp pain in her stomach. She knew it was wrong of her to lie to her mother and lead her to believe something that wasn't true. She didn't know when she'd become so selfish, thinking only of herself, but she had dug herself too deep in the hole to stop.

"Yes, Mother," she replied instead. "I will wed Lord Blackwell, and he will protect us all."

And with that, she hugged her mother and Morgana farewell and walked outside, climbed onto the stallion, and both Marietta and Lord Cross disappeared into the darkness.

"I THOUGHT YOU SAID THERE WAS A TOWN HERE!" Marietta shouted toward Cross when they finally arrived in Valeria.

The magical and lawless free town that Lord Cross had boasted about for the past two days turned out to be nothing but a barren dirt land, even worse than Hibernia, which Marietta never thought would be possible.

Cross rubbed the back of his neck. "There is! I mean,

there was, at least. I've been here before. I know Valeria exists. I'm just not sure what happened."

Marietta threw her arms in the air. "Great, I left my family back home just to come to a town that doesn't even exist!" She kicked a pile of rocks, dust flying across the air.

Cross waved the particles away from his face as they flew at him. "I'm starting to think that maybe a completely lawless land isn't exactly as great as it sounds." He turned to Marietta. "But, hey, we didn't leave Marsonia just to come here. Who cares if Valeria doesn't exist? It's just a minor obstacle in our journey. A night or two here, and we'll be on our way to our next location." He grabbed her hands and held them tight. "Besides, it's you and me, remember? As long as we have each other, no amount of obstacles is strong enough to stop us."

Marietta took a deep breath at his words and tried to calm herself down. He was right. This journey wasn't about Valeria. It wasn't about arriving in a ghost town. It was about their new life together, and getting so frustrated so fast wasn't going to help anyone.

"You're absolutely right, Cross. I apologize for over-reacting."

He smiled, then brushed her hair aside and kissed her. "It's okay," he said. "I still like you. Now, come on, let's go see if we can find any people."

They explored the small town, stepping over piles of ashes and potholes imprinted on the roads. Marietta felt spoiled for being able to live in a town like Hibernia, especially compared to this toxic dump they were stepping into. There were puddles of black tar lining the roads, carcasses littered the side-walks, and what resembled dried blood stains on the piles of dead fallen trees.

"I don't think anyone lives here," Marietta said after an hour of walking. "Even if someone did, I doubt they'd be able to survive for long. There's just nothing here." She picked up a bloody rag and sniffed. "Yeah, that's definitely been here awhile." She tossed it back down onto the ground.

"Maybe," Cross agreed. "But since we're here, we may as well try and find some shelter. It's too dark to go anywhere else. The next town isn't for another fifty miles."

Suddenly, a loud scream came from a distance. It was a piercing shriek, enough to send chills up Marietta's body. Her vampire senses were strong, and she could smell the body the voice was coming from.

"This way," she said to Cross, pointing to her left.

"How do you know?"

"Trust me. I know."

They made several wrong turns, but eventually, they found a young woman and man, roughly the same age as Marietta and Cross, huddled beside a pile of twigs, arms wrapped around each other, and shaking.

Being the gentleman that he was, Lord Cross quickly rushed over. "Are you okay?" he asked.

Marietta wasn't far behind, and when she caught up to him, she saw the two strangers nodding.

"There... there was a wolf. We were out gathering supplies, and it tackled us, ripping everything out of our hands," the woman said. She looked over at the man. "Sorry, honey, I guess it's another night of starvation."

Marietta desperately wanted to leave before the wolf came back to feed on one of them. She tried to discreetly tug on Cross' sleeve, but he stayed put.

Instead, he knelt down in front of the man and woman. "My name's Cross, and this here is Marietta. What are your names?"

The woman looked at the man before turning back to Cross. "I'm Florence, and this is my brother, Claude."

Do you two live here?" Cross asked.

They nodded.

"Where is everyone?" he asked again. "The last time I was here, it was prosperous, full of people laughing and enjoying life. I was expecting it to be the same. How could a land free from laws and dictatorship crumble so quickly? I thought I was going crazy at first."

Florence shook her head. "You're not going crazy, and you're right. There used to be a lot of people here. But then things got out of hand. Without laws, people started killing each other, taking what belonged to others as their own. It got so bad that people started fleeing for their lives. No one remained unscathed from the rebels that overtook Valeria. Claude and I are only still here because we built a shack in the middle of the woods years ago that no one else knows about. We've been hiding there ever since, coming out to search for food every now and then, seeing no one else but wild animals. In fact, you two are the first human beings we've encountered in over a year."

"Shelter?" Marietta blurted out, then covered her mouth when Cross shot a look at her.

She knew that had been rude, but she was so tired from the lack of sleep and constant walking that she just wanted a place to lie down and rest.

"Yes, we have a place in the woods. It's not much, but if you two want, you're welcome to stay with us. I don't think there's anyone else in this town that will find us and hurt us."

"That sounds... amazing, actually. We really just need one good night's rest, and we'll be on our way. But are you sure you trust us? How are you so sure we're not out to hurt you?"

Marietta nudged Cross hard in the side of his stomach. He winced, but ignored her.

"We trust you," Claude spoke up. "We're pretty good at reading people, and we know you don't have any ill intentions toward us."

Lord Cross smiled. "Well, *we* graciously appreciate your

offer," he said, gesturing to himself and Marietta. "And in exchange for your humble kindness, we would like to offer you some food and supplies in return, as a gratitude for your generosity."

Marietta nudged him again. This time, he wasn't so kind.

"Marietta, darling, Florence and Claude here are nice enough to provide us shelter for the night. Don't you think we owe it to them to share what we have with them also?"

Marietta shrugged, feeling embarrassed and ashamed. "Sorry," she whispered.

"Don't sweat it," Florence reassured. "Even if you don't decide to share with us, we're happy to help anyway."

As Cross and Marietta followed Florence and Claude across town and into the woods, Marietta couldn't help but sense danger nearby. She could smell it. Someone, or something, was lurking in the woods. Part of her felt like she should've said something, but all she wanted at the moment was to lie down on something other than dirt. She didn't want to be bothered with anything else now. Whatever it was, she'd deal with it tomorrow.

LATER THAT NIGHT, MARIETTA FOUND HERSELF lying on top of a thin mattress with Cross by her side. She had never been on the same bed with a man before, only her mother, and she felt nervous being there with him.

"What's wrong?" he asked her, the fingers from one of his hands stroking her hair.

"Oh, it's nothing, just a little nervous, that's all. I've never been in bed with a man before."

Cross chuckled. "You think I'm going to hurt you or something? Don't be nervous, Marietta. I'm not my brother." He leaned over and kissed her on the forehead.

"It's not just that, I guess." Marietta then said.

A look of concern washed over Cross' face. "What else is bothering you, my dear? Is it home? Do you miss your mother?"

She shook her head. "No, well, I do, but it's not that. I just have a strange feeling that we're being watched." She turned to look at him. "Am I just being paranoid?"

"I think you're just tired. We're safe; there's no one else. This place is top secret, remember? There's no way anyone can find us." This time, he kissed her on the lips. "Trust me, everything is fine. Nothing to worry about."

"Do you promise?" Marietta asked.

"I promise." Cross kissed her again, leaning her back against the mattress and sliding a hand up her blouse.

He kissed her passionately, their tongues entangled in a dance as he brushed her neck with his lips.

"Your lips feel so warm, and your skin is so soft," he whispered into her ear.

His hand now traveled further up her top. He lifted it over her shoulders and then removed the skirt she wore around her legs, until she was completely naked in front of him. Cross turned his fingers into a camera and took a mental picture of her.

"Click." He smiled. "An image of perfection. How do you feel?"

Marietta blushed. "I... I feel so vulnerable. Will it hurt?"

He smiled again and shook his head. "Maybe a little, but trust me, the pleasure you'll feel will make you not even remember the pain." He climbed over on top of her. "Marietta, darling, you are the most beautiful woman in all of Marsonia, possibly the most beautiful woman in the entire world. I want to be the fruits for your children. I want to live the rest of my life with you by my side. Forget about Blackwell. With someone like you with me, it's a guarantee that I will be crowned the next king of Marsonia."

And just like that, Marietta and Cross made love, their bodies pressed close together in pure intimacy.

Several hours later, Marietta had her arms wrapped around Lord Cross. His muscles and toned body were impeccable, a true vision of manhood, and it made Marietta swoon for him.

"How do you feel now?" he asked, winking at her.

She blushed, "Like a true woman."

Just then, they heard a loud bang, followed by what sounded like Florence's scream. They both threw on their clothes and rushed out of the room, only to find Florence and Claude kneeling on the ground, their hands behind their bodies. In front of them were three masked men, each one holding a gun to their heads.

Marietta gasped, turning the men's attention to her and Cross.

"Take care of them," one of the men said to the other two as he walked toward where Marietta and Cross were standing.

With two quick fires from the guns of the other two men, Florence and Claude collapsed onto the ground, blood pouring from their bodies, rendering them lifeless.

I knew I heard something earlier, Marietta thought, kicking herself for not speaking up sooner. Now, she was lucky if they made it out of this alive.

"Down on the ground, now! Unless you want to end up like your friends over there." The man pointed his gun at them, Cross quickly falling to his knees.

Marietta followed suit, but she couldn't help but wonder how she could easily stop them, destroy them. Suck out everything from inside them. But that would also expose what she really was to Cross. She looked over at him, sweat pouring down his face.

Is my reputation really worth us getting killed?

"Now, give us everything you have. Coins, food, everything." The man demanded, with the other two wiping themselves off from the blood of Florence and Claude and joining him.

"But, my good man, how about we give you half? We have a long journey ahead of us, and if we give them all to you, what will we have left for ourselves?"

That was a mistake from Cross. The man spat a tooth out onto the wooden floor and touched his gun to Cross' head.

"And what makes you think we give a rat's ass about your survival? It's every man for himself, you foolish rich boy. What happened? Daddy get mad at you and take away your inheritance?" The three of them joined in laughter, their breaths reeking of alcohol, reminding Marietta of Lord Blackwell. They were so similar, and soon, all the anger came rushing back.

In one swift motion, Marietta stood up on her feet and charged toward the man pointing the gun. She sunk her claws into his warm flesh and sucked him dry, the taste of his blood sending a sensation through her body. It felt magnificent.

The other two men backed away, their eyes wide in terror. Marietta could have just let them go free, but that would only risk them telling others about her. Who knows how many of them there were?

Approaching one of the two, she grabbed the one closest to her, sinking her fangs into his veins and allowing the delicious blood to course down her throat. He didn't taste as good as the first, but it was still much better than the loaves of bread she had survived on over the past few days.

Screaming, the last masked man tried to run away, his hands fidgeting with the doorknob and trying to pull it open. But before he could open it, Marietta grabbed a knife from off the table and threw it at him. The knife pierced through his shoulder and into the wooden door, causing him to scream in agony.

She finished off the man she was holding, threw him on top of the first intruder, and made her way toward the third. She grabbed him by the hair.

"Why are you here?" she demanded. "How did you find us? Did Azra send you?"

The man was trembling, his body coming close to wetting his pants. "Azra? Who? What? We just wanted food. I swear. Please, don't kill me!"

"I don't believe you." Marietta gripped tighter. "Who SENT you?" she demanded again.

"No one! Oh, god, it hurts. Please, just kill me already if you won't let me go. I already told you. We saw you talking to those two." He pointed to where Florence and Claude were lying. "We heard that you had food. So, we followed you to steal it. That's it, I swear."

"Darling, I think he's telling the truth," Cross said, still on the ground.

"Quiet!" she shrieked.

Then she looked at the man again. There was blood dripping down his back from where the knife made its mark. Marietta contemplated letting him go, to at least show Cross that she had some sort of humanity left in her, but the smell was so tantalizing that her mouth couldn't resist salivating.

She licked her lips, her eyes wide with hunger. She tried to stop her mouth from inching toward him, but she couldn't resist. His scent was just too strong. She tried to think of Cross, hoping a reminder of him would retreat her fangs, but they only grew sharper. Saliva dripping, she sunk her fatal teeth into his neck, slurping and swallowing to her heart's content. The blood was sweet, but to her, it tasted bitter. She wasn't sure whether it was the guilt of betraying Cross or whether his blood was tainted. Either way, she continued to drain him until he became pale.

When she threw the final body on top of the pile, she looked over at Lord Cross, who had a mask of terror over his face. He was speechless. But Marietta didn't blame him. If she saw the person she had just consummated intimacy with suck the blood out of three people, she'd be a little terrified, too.

She knelt down and touched her lover's arm. He flinched back.

"They won't be bothering us anymore," she whispered. "We're safe now."

"You're... You're...," Cross stuttered. "You're one of them, one of the demons." He backed away into a corner, afraid to let Marietta come near him.

"A vampire, yes. Like my father. The man your family burned."

"You're... Vladimir's daughter? The one we've been searching for?"

Marietta nodded. "Yes, but I'm not a monster, I swear. My father wasn't either. Just hungry and misunderstood. Sure, we kill, but most of the time, we're vigilantes. We only kill for good. My father killed to help the Hibernians, and I killed to save us. Don't you understand? I'm not as evil as you all think!"

But Lord Cross remained silent, his hands still wrapped around his arms for self-protection.

"Cross, please, you know me. You know I'm not evil. I'm just... a little different from the rest of you."

"Is that how you got over the wall and into Castle Vesunna? With your... your... strange... super powers? God, it's even difficult to say! These kinds of things are only supposed to exist in stories, not in real life."

Marietta rested a hand on his shoulder. This time, he didn't flinch. "Yes, being a vampire helped me get into Castle

Vesunna. But I had to! For you. For us! It was the only way I could prevent myself from marrying Lord Blackwell."

Cross glared at her. "And how do I know you won't kill me? Like you did to those three over there?"

"Because, Cross. Because I love you. I could never hurt you like that."

"You... you love me?"

Marietta nodded. "Ever since I first laid eyes on you, I can't stop thinking about you. And when you told me you felt the same way, my world just felt complete. I wouldn't want to do anything to let that all fall apart."

A small smile slowly formed on his face. "Darling, I love you, too."

"Queen Azra, your highness. I have terrible news!" Nicolo called out while running into Azra's corridor, where he found her perched on top of her throne.

"Nicolo, Nicolo, Nicolo. I'm surprised your behavior has become so rash. You should know better than to just rush in here without knocking. Don't you know that doing so can get you killed?"

Nicolo nodded. "Yes, I understand, your highness. But I have terrible news that I must share with you this instant!"

Queen Azra yawned. "Haven't you learned your lesson from the last time, Nicolo? If someone is trying to sneak across the wall, inform the guards. I have much more important things to do than worry about every last imbecile who tries to cross the impossible."

Nicolo shook his head. "No, your highness, it's not that at all. It's worse, much worse."

Queen Azra yawned again. "Alright, fine, what is this terribly awful news you can't wait to tell me about?"

"Lord Cross is gone, and Lord Blackwell is dead." Nicolo spat, causing the queen to drop the chalice she was holding, the glass shattering all over the marble floor.

"Who?! Who did this?! Who killed my precious boy? I need answers, now!" the queen demanded. "Find him. You are not to rest until you find the one responsible! Do you understand me?"

Nicolo quickly nodded. "Your highness, I know who is responsible."

"Well, don't just stand there with your mouth closed. Spit it out!"

"It was... it was the peasant girl, Marietta, the poor girl from Hibernia who was supposed to wed Lord Blackwell. I saw her climbing out of Lord Blackwell's window. I have reason to believe she's an abnormal, much like Vladimir Covici, her father. I also have reason to believe that she is responsible for the murder of Augustus and Benedict, the guards who were guarding the wall."

"And Cross?"

"I saw Cross leave with her, on his stallion. He may be in danger. She may be holding him captive." Nicolo finished.

"And where did they go?" Queen Azra asked, her tone growing tenser, and her face growing more and more red.

"I'm... I'm not sure, your highness."

"Well, don't just stand there like a blubbering idiot. Go find them!" The queen ordered, her voice loud enough to shake the entire castle.

Azra sunk back onto her throne as she watched Nicolo dash out of the room. She didn't know where she had gone wrong. Her entire life, all she ever wanted was to give the people what was best for them. She moved to Marsonia, set up her kingdom, and drew the dividing line between the rich and the poor to avoid having bad influences befall upon her children. She believed that if she kept Luceria closed off from the

Hibernians, then her two sons might actually have a chance to live prosperous lives.

But it was all for nothing. Her eldest, Blackwell, decided to fall in love with a peasant girl, choosing her over all the other high-class ladies he could've had. Foolish, foolish boy. And now look at him, shriveled up inside a midnight black sack, soon to be taken to the crematorium.

She sighed. *I taught him everything I could. Where did I go so wrong? And if that poor peasant girl was able to do so much already, imagine how much she would've destroyed the kingdom if she had become the new queen. No, that would've been too much to bear.*

But in reality, Marietta reminded Queen Azra of herself, how she used to be a poor peasant girl, hungry for power and revenge. She was born Azra Romanov, daughter to a merchant father, Mikhail, living in the small town of Sortavala in Russia. It was a scenic town by the border of Finland, with snowy mountains and picturesque cabins, perfect for cold winter days. However, the Russians and the Finnish have always had disagreements on where the dividing line truly was, both sides claiming Sortavala as their own territory and doing whatever possible to take it for themselves.

When the Russians refused to concede, the Finnish invaded Sortavala, killed many of residents who lived there, and took all the women as slaves. Little Azra watched in horror as her mother was being taken away, while her father tried to pull her away and go into hiding. She was only six years old, and that was the last time she ever saw her mother.

A few years later, her father remarried, to none other than a Finnish woman, Livia Korhonen. Azra tried to object, tried to warn her father that their people killed her mother, but Mikhail refused to listen, pushing Azra aside as he remained blinded by love. It didn't take long until Livia decided to put her devious plan into action.

One day, Azra came home from school and found her father lying dead in their home, with Livia holding a knife and sitting on a kitchen chair. Surrounding her, were bags and bags of her father's riches, all neatly packed and ready for their journey.

"You belong to me now, you little brat." Azra remembered her saying before she dragged her out of the home.

"Daddy! No!" Azra cried out for her father, trying to fight her way to him, but Livia was much too strong.

For nearly fifteen years, Azra lived under Livia's roof and was treated like a slave, pushed around and beat while she waited on Livia hand and foot, and was never given more than mere crumbs to eat.

At the age twenty-five, Livia remarried once again, this time, to the king of Finland, King Eetu. He had a son of his own, Jouko, and Jouko found great interest in Azra, pleading his father to enforce an executive order in which Azra was forced to wed Jouko. But Azra refused. She tried to run away, escape, whatever she could to avoid marrying him as she found him even more repulsive than she found Livia. But as a slave, she had no say in who she could or could not wed, and two short months later, they were married.

But Azra's story didn't end there. She wasn't forced to live a life of misery. Two years later, at the age of twenty-seven, Azra discovered that she was... different from the others. She felt a tingling sensation coming from the necklace her mother had given her as a child, her senses forced into overdrive, and she discovered that she had the ability to curse others. She didn't believe it at first, trying it out on one of the guards and turning him into a pig. It worked!

With her newfound power, she contemplated hiding it and using it only for good, but the rage that had built up inside her for over twenty years prevented her from doing so, corrupting her mind and making her hungry for revenge and murder.

One night, while in bed with her husband, Prince Jouko, massaging his feet and feeding him grapes, she decided to take her plan into action. With just a few simple chants and waves of her fingers, she soon witnessed Prince Jouko dissolving before her very eyes. Azra was left laughing at the scene.

She felt no remorse, no pity, and proceeded to liquify both Livia and Eetu. She wanted to get the hell out of Finland, run as far away as possible and never look back, leaving all her painful memories behind. She ran and ran, further and further south, until she finally reached Romania, only to fall ill. An elderly woman eventually found her lying in the dirt road and took her home to care for her. When Azra awakened, the woman informed her that she fainted because she was extremely malnourished, terrible for someone who was carrying a child.

"I'm... I'm with child?" Azra stuttered, her ears struggling to believe even her own words.

The woman nodded in confirmation. "Yes, twins, actually."

And that's when Azra's life started to take form. Despite carrying the spawns of Jouko, she vowed to never treat her children the way she had been treated. She vowed to not only be the greatest mother, but also the greatest leader, to all of Romania, to provide everyone with a life of luxury and fortune. But like all plans go, hers did not turn out the way she had expected. When it was finally time for her to deliver, she went into the slums of Romania to meet with the only doctor who was willing to deliver her babies free of charge. Blackwell was first, his delivery full of ease and was pain-free. However, when it came time for Cross, Azra began bleeding profusely. The doctor, with his lack of medical knowledge, didn't know what the issue was or how to stop it, so Azra was left to bleed out while he pulled Cross out from her. Luckily, Cross came out fine, but Azra passed out from the blood loss and was out for nearly two weeks. And although the doctor told her she was incredibly lucky and could've died, all she could hear was how he almost killed her. She grabbed her two newborn sons and stormed off, vowing to never return to the slums.

A year later, Azra finally made her way into Marsonia. She had initially wanted to become ruler of all of Romania, but even with her supernatural powers, she struggled to overturn the current king, traveling south instead to the free land of Marsonia, and the rest was history. She had tried to also overtake Valeria, the independent town next door, but by the time she got there, Valeria was already too far gone, people murdering each other for play in a town that rotted away more and more every day.

"Marietta needs to be stopped," Queen Azra whispered to herself when her mind returned to the present. "If she isn't, Luceria, and perhaps the world, will soon be destroyed."

BUILDING A SHELTER IN THE DEEP WOODS PROVED not so helpful when the high queen was on a rampage looking for someone who lived there. Desdemona and Morgana had to find that out the hard way. Unbeknownst to them, it turned out that Marietta wasn't actually at Castle Vesunna with Lord Blackwell, as she had informed them. In fact, Marietta Covici murdered Lord Blackwell and was now currently on the run with his brother.

As Desdemona placed the last of the dishes on the table, ready for another night of supper, the front door flew open. Nicolo, along with five other armed guards, were standing there, ready to take down anyone who refused to listen.

"Is this the residence of Marietta Covici?" he asked.

"It is," Desdemona stepped in while Morgana hid in the kitchen. "And who might you be?"

Without saying a word, the man extended an arm and handed a letter to Desdemona, who grabbed a candelabra from the nightstand so she could read it.

"No, it can't be...," she whispered. "The queen..."

"...needs to see Marietta. Immediately," he finished.

"But I don't understand. Marietta went to Castle Vesunna just a few days ago to be with Lord Blackwell," Desdemona probed.

"Marietta Covici is not only not present at the castle, but she has also murdered Lord Blackwell. She is under arrest, and we need to take her to Castle Vesunna immediately to face her punishment."

Desdemona nearly fainted. She couldn't believe what she was hearing. Morgana rushed to her side to keep her from collapsing onto the ground. "My daughter... my precious little girl... a murderer? No, it can't be."

"Well, it is," Nicolo continued. "Now, I'm afraid you'll have to let us in, ma'am, so we can search the premise. Otherwise, we'll be forced to let ourselves in. Marietta Covici is under arrest for the murder of Lord Blackwell. We must take her in to see Queen Azra to face the consequences, or your entire family will be killed," he repeated, the second time no less shocking to Desdemona.

"You may come in if you like, but like she said, Marietta is not here. If she isn't at the castle, then I have no idea about her whereabouts." Morgana spoke for her friend, fanning her to keep her from passing out.

Nicolo wore a look of disbelief. "Well, tell me this, then. If Marietta is an abnormal, and apparently, her father was an abnormal, what does that make you?" He inched closer to her. "If you had any sense of intellect, you'd know that abnormals get burned in this town. Are you ready to face your death?"

Morgana gasped. "Death?! What? Desdemona, what is he talking about? What's an abnormal?"

Desdemona waved a hand at Morgana. "It's okay, Morgana. I can handle this." Then she faced her friend. "I should've told you years ago, warned you about what could potentially happen if you let us stay with you, but I had no other choice. I had to keep us safe. Marietta is a vampire. Her father was one, and he was killed shortly before we ran into you." Then she turned back to Nicolo. "But I'm human, one hundred percent human, not an abnormal. You have to believe me."

While Morgana was still left to process the news she had just received, Nicolo let out a loud laugh. "You really expect me to believe that in a family of abnormals, you're human? Ha! That's the biggest lie I've ever heard. Guards, seize her!"

"What?! No! Stop! This is a mistake! I'm human, I swear. Morgana, tell them! Tell them you've known me my whole life and that I'm human," Desdemona pleaded.

But to her surprise, Morgana did not utter a single word. She remained quiet, emotionless, unconcerned that the guards of Luceria had just slit her best friend's throat and were now dragging her away.

"Cross, say something, please! This silence is killing me," Marietta pleaded back at the cabin while Cross paced around the room in complete silence.

He continued to ignore her.

"Please, just talk to me!" she pleaded again.

"What?! What am I supposed to say, Marietta?" He stopped pacing and turned to face her.

His face was red, and his nostrils were flaring. "How in the bloody hell am I supposed to find out that you're a damn vampire and just pretend like everything's okay? How, Marietta? Tell me!"

And then his mind clicked, and he came to a sudden realization. He knelt down in front of her and slowly asked, hoping to receive an answer he didn't want in response. "Marietta, when you came into my room that night and told me that you took care of Blackwell, what *exactly* did you mean? Did you do something to him? Because now, after finding out what you're capable of, I'm starting to doubt that you two just talked. I know my brother very well, and he does not do well with just talking."

"I didn't do anything," Marietta lied. "We *did* just talk."

"Bullshit, Marietta! Stop lying to me! God! I don't even know what to believe anyone. It's like every word that comes out of your mouth is a damn lie!" He paused, looked over at the pile of corpses still lying there, and whispered. "Did you... did you kill him, suck out his blood, also?"

"Cross, please, you know me! Why would I do that?" Marietta tried to deflect, but she knew that Lord Cross wouldn't buy it.

"Stop lying, Marietta. Just. Stop. LYING!"

She bowed her head to the ground and nodded in shame. "I did," she whispered. "I killed Lord Blackwell."

Cross kicked his foot against the wooden door to their bedroom, his foot leaving a small crack in it. "I can't believe this!" He turned to Marietta and pointed to himself. "I trusted you. I loved you, and I trusted you. And this, this is how you repay me? How could I have been so stupid to run off with a killer?"

"But I'm not a killer, Cross. I love you, and I know that a part of you still loves me, too." Tears were now flowing from her eyes. She didn't even bother holding them back because she was well aware that she had gone too far. There was no turning back now. She tried embracing Cross, tried calming him down so she could explain herself, but he only pushed her away.

"No, Marietta, you *are* a killer, and no, I *don't* love you." He grabbed his overcoat, walked out the door, and rode away on his stallion, leaving Marietta there all alone.

Five

It took Marietta nearly six days before she finally arrived back at her home in Hibernia. After Lord Cross had left her in the Valeria wilderness, she walked several days before finding a fisherman who graciously gave her a ride back to Hibernia on his boat. She was starving and malnourished by this point, seeing absolutely nothing and no one during her journey, only insects and snakes, none of which were enough to satisfy her. She could've had her way with the fisherman, drain him and steal his boat, but by that point, she had become so weak that she knew she wouldn't be able to fight off the burly fisherman even if she tried. Plus, he was kind enough to share with her his fish and broth. She wasn't that much of a monster who would kill such a kind and caring man.

But going home wasn't as easy as hopping on a boat. The dock of Luceria was now much more heavily guarded, shooting anyone who came within a hundred-mile radius on the Black Sea. There was no chance that the fisherman would be able to pull up to land without risking his own life. And because they couldn't even get close enough, Marietta's abilities were useless.

Their only other option was to travel inland, straight into the Danube River and across the mossy waters of the Vătafu-Lunguleț Reserve, where Marietta would have to trek on feet the rest of the way through the isolated wilderness and back into Hibernia. She was determined, but her body was also failing her, so the fisherman gave her the rest of his food before saying farewell and departing.

And so, Marietta continued her journey alone, fighting off swampy creatures and the numerous natural disasters in the area. She wanted to give up. Oh, she wanted to give up many times, but the thought of seeing her mother again kept her going. Another eight days later, she finally made it back to Morgana's cabin.

"Mother! I'm home!" she shouted as she walked through the front door, her garments dripping wet from the harsh rain just a few moments ago.

However, her mother wasn't there to greet her, only Morgana, who sat in the kitchen and wept.

"Morgana? What's wrong? Where's Mother?" Marietta asked.

Morgana jumped, startled. "Marietta, what are you doing

here?" She hopped up from her chair and scurried away from the girl. "Stay... Stay away from me. Don't hurt me!"

"What? Morgana, what are you talking about? Why would I hurt you? Where's Mother?" She inched closer to Morgana.

"Don't!" Morgana shouted, pointing a finger at Marietta. "Don't come any closer. I know what you are and what you did. I want you out of my house. Immediately!"

"Morgana, please, you're not making any sense."

This time, Morgana held a kitchen knife in front of her, pointing it at Marietta. "The guards came by, you little freak. You murdered Lord Blackwell, and you're... you're... some kind of supernatural freak! I want you out of my house, now!"

Marietta couldn't say she was surprised. She didn't really leave clean tracks or cover up her steps. She knew they'd find out sooner or later what she did. She had just hoped they didn't.

"Where's Mother? I'm not leaving without Mother."

Morgana shook her head. "Gone, my child. Dead. They took her. Slaughtered her and took her. She's just like you, a freak. You both deserve to die."

"Mother...," Marietta whispered. "No, not Mother." She turned to Morgana, raising her voice, "But she's human!"

"Even so, she gave birth to a monster. She deserved to die. I should've never let the two of you into my home. You've both done nothing but bring me trouble. Doesn't matter, anyway. She's gone. Saw them slit her throat right in front of me."

"She's your best friend!" Marietta shouted. "Don't you care that she's gone?"

"I feel nothing."

Just then, there was a knock on the door. Marietta's heart jumped, the dread of the guards coming to claim her returning to her thoughts. She ran behind the stairwell and hid while Morgana opened the door.

"Miss Morgana, nice seeing you again," the man at the door said as he greeted her. "I got a little tip that young Marietta Covici has returned home. I'd like to speak with her, please."

Oh, no, the guards. How? What? Who told them? No, it can't be. The fisherman? A thousand thoughts coursed through Marietta's mind. She didn't know who she could trust anymore.

"The little brat is under the stairwell." Morgana was quick to give her up, just like she was quick to let them take away Desdemona.

Was she a woman of no remorse? She'd always hated the Lucerians. Why was she now helping them? It all didn't make sense. Who was she, really?

At those words, Marietta slowly came out from beneath the stairwell and surrendered herself. She looked over at Morgana, who had a stern look of dissatisfaction on her face but was still nervously rubbing her hands together in sweat. She refused to look her in the eyes, glancing around the room suspiciously as if her eyes were begging for asylum from the man. It was in that moment that she knew.

Morgana had tipped them off, informing the guards of Marietta's return. Marietta knew Morgana couldn't be trusted, right from the very start, but her mother had insisted that they stay with her. Look where that got her now. Marietta growled and threw herself against the woman like a tornado knocking down a row of houses. They both rolled against the hardwood, flailing their arms at each other, before suddenly stopping at the door when the man walked in. Now that she was closer, Marietta recognized him as Nicolo, the same man Cross entrusted. A double betrayal, all in one night.

She watched in defeat as Nicolo ordered his army to drag

Marietta away, tossing aside some furniture and clothing that stood in their way.

"Morgana! Morgana! Don't let them take me, please! Stop them!" she cried out to Morgana, who could only stare at her in disapproval and disgust as she closed the door behind them.

It wasn't until she reached the footsteps of the castle that she realized Morgana had not gone after her. She cried out bitter tears, but the men showed her no remorse. Nicolo, in particular, simply looked revolted and on the verge of attacking her at any minute. Oh, such irony that she was the one they were mad at when they worked as slaves to a ruthless tyrant.

It wasn't until they reached the steps of Queen Azra's tower did Marietta realize what her punishment was going to be. She tried to kick and scream, anything she could to escape her impending fate, but the more she struggled, the more she was held back with greater strength until her skin turned purple and her breath staggered.

"Your Majesty," was all she could say upon being thrown at the queen's feet, blood spilling from her mouth.

Queen Azra knelt down beside the lowly peasant, lifting her gaunt chin and glaring into her eyes. "You have made a grave mistake by killing Lord Blackwell."

Marietta spat out blood onto the ground. "He deserved it."

She tried to avoid the queen's gaze, but there was something about the way her green eyes pierced through her with intent, a sudden glow that swam through her limbs and made it impossible for her to move, almost as if her limbs were made of lead.

Queen Azra's movements were mesmerizing, like she was hypnotizing her, an aura expelling from her that seemed too manipulative to be human.

What is she? Marietta thought as the pain inside her mind pierced against her eyes.

"What have you done to me?" she screamed.

"Are you ready to tell us what happened?" the queen asked.

Marietta's body was vigorously trembling, but she still remained paralyzed. Queen Azra simply stood there, her long dark hair flowing against the cold winter breeze. Marietta glanced over at Nicolo, who stood beside the queen, emotionless, with Lord Cross stepping outside with them, a grim look on his pale face.

Marietta looked over at Lord Cross. "You. This is all your fault!"

But before Cross could speak for himself, Queen Azra stepped in. "On the contrary, my young dear. I have been onto you for quite a while now. Ah, such a resemblance to Vladimir Covici. I've been keeping tabs on you, every step you took and every move you made. You and your mother. You both thought you were so clever, hiding from me in the forest, but what you two fools didn't realize, however, was that I have eyes everywhere."

She whistled, and at that, Morgana stepped out.

"Morgana?" Marietta asked. "What are you doing here? You said you hated the queen!"

"On the contrary again, my child. Morgana here actually works for me. You see, she is of high class; her parents once served as my loyal guards. I sent her to live in Hibernia for the sole purpose of finding you and isolating you to a place where I could track you at all times. And well, it was just my lucky day that she happened to know your poor, stupid mother."

"My mother is *not* stupid! Take that back!" Marietta shouted. Then she turned to Morgana, "Morgana, how could you do this? How could you betray Mother like this?"

"Betray your mother?" Morgana repeated. "You two kept

this secret from me for over ten years, and *I'm* the traitor? You really need to start taking responsibility for your own actions, Marietta, or you'll end up dead, just like your mother." She spat on the ground beside Marietta and retreated inside.

Marietta fell to her knees. She couldn't bear the physical and emotional pain she was experiencing. She felt so trapped, so hopeless. She was only trying to protect herself, and now, there was no one left to save her. She wanted to escape, tear them all apart with her teeth and let the blood spill on the floor. She wanted to decimate each and every single one of them. If only she could get to the queen's throat, she'd be able to declare herself as the new leader. Azra's once-loyal guards will all bow down to her.

"She's not going to speak. Finish her," Queen Azra ordered her guards.

"Wait, stop!" Marietta called out as they raised their swords. "I'm pregnant!"

Marietta wasn't sure before, blaming the nausea and stomach pains on her lack of nourishment and lethargy. But when she began experiencing morning sickness morning after morning, and her menstrual cycle never came when it usually comes on time, she started to suspect something.

Queen Azra let out an obnoxious laugh. "Ha! And what makes you think I care? Just because you've been promiscuous doesn't mean I should spare you your life."

"Oh, I think you'll want to," Marietta said sternly, fully knowing that she had only ever been with one person.

The expression on the queen's face quickly changed. "And what makes you say that?"

"Because I'm pregnant with your grandchild." She sneered and looked over at Lord Cross. "That's right, you're a father."

Fuming, Azra turned to her son. "Cross, tell me this isn't true. Tell me you aren't the father of this bastard child."

Marietta bent her head down and smiled. She knew that

confessing her pregnancy would help the queen take pity on her and let her go. After all, it *was* her son's fault that she was now in this mess. If it wasn't for his persistence and him coming onto her, this would've never happened.

But to her surprise, Cross denied it. "It's not mine," he said nonchalantly, causing Marietta to shoot a glare of daggers at him."

"What? Liar!" she shouted. "He's lying! Lord Cross *is* the father of my unborn child! Why are you lying? Tell them the truth! Tell them how much you love me!"

But Cross refused to look his former lover in the eye. Instead, he looked up at the sky, his confession even more shocking than his denial. "No, Marietta, I've never loved you. I was only with you for a brief period of time because I wanted to be king. I knew that if I stole my brother's bride, then I'd be blessed with the title. But it doesn't matter anymore. With him gone, the throne is as good as mine. Right, Mother?" He turned to the queen, who nodded at his question. Then he turned to Marietta. "And that child, definitely not mine. I don't know who you've been with, but I want nothing to do with it. And I want nothing to do with you. Hear my words, Marietta Covici, I do not love you."

Livid with rage that the man she once loved used her for his own benefit and was now betraying her, she quickly lunged forward at him. However, Queen Azra got to her first, sending her trapped in midair.

No, it can't be.

"What are you?" she shouted in terror.

The queen could only laugh, the kind of laugh that was enough to cut through skin and make blood boil. Her eyes then flashed red, and that alone terrified Marietta.

"Oh, Marietta, Marietta. You really thought the Covici family was the only abnormal in town? No, darling. You see, I am part of the Romanov Ravens."

Marietta gulped. *You're... you're a witch?*

The Ravens were the most notorious criminals of the 16th Century, wreaking havoc on the entire European continent, and the vampires' worst nightmare.

"Yes, my dear. Yes, I am, a descendent of the same blood."

What? Did I say that out loud? Marietta thought again.

That's when Azra leaned in much closer, her necklace dangling in front of Marietta's face. It looked like a cheap rusty trinket that belonged in the dump, not around someone's neck.

"No, but I can still hear you," the queen whispered.

Her face formed a cruel smile as she moved her hands around Marietta's body. "You see, my stupid child, there's a reason why no one has ever tried to take down a Raven. They simply couldn't. You vampires all think you're so powerful." She turned around and spat at Marietta. "You're nothing, filled with greed and ignorance, thinking you're powerful enough to seize whatever you want."

"Are you going to kill me?"

Queen Azra cackled. "I could, but what fun would that be? Lucky for you, I'm feeling a little... charitable tonight, you know, since it has now come to my attention that you are with child. I never really liked Blackwell anyway, such a spoiled little brat. How about I make you a deal and let you choose? Either you die now, or a curse shall befall upon your unborn child, as karma for killing instead of wedding your husband. The answer may prove more challenging than you think. If I were you, I'd think very carefully before making a decision."

But Marietta didn't want to think. She just wanted to get the hell out of her nightmare situation, to run as far away as possible and live her life in solitude. She didn't care about her bastard child, and she hated Cross for abandoning her in her time of need.

"I choose freedom," she whispered.

"Very well, may your selfishness befall a curse upon your descendant, a curse that will leave the child with a face no one could ever love so that another heart shall be spared from being broken," Queen Azra confirmed and touched Marietta's forehead.

Marietta's head began to spin, and when she tried to open her mouth, all that came out was silence. And everything went dark.

~

IT WASN'T UNTIL SHE MET THE LOVE OF HER LIFE months later that she realized how evil the queen had been.

The curse hadn't touched her. She still felt the same as she had before killing Lord Blackwell, her abilities still intact. But she felt something in her blood begin to change, something evil.

After leaving Castle Vesunna, Marietta was banished to live in isolation in the town of Valeria. With no family and no resources, she was forced to survive off of whatever wild animal came her way, tearing them apart and ravaging their flesh to prevent her child from dying. She didn't want the child, a forever reminder of Lord Cross, but she knew she also couldn't abandon it. It wasn't the child's fault that Marietta now lived in misery. It was her own fault.

One evening, as she sat in her shoddily-built cabin, she heard a noise outside. She rushed out, prepared to destroy whoever was trying to break in. But she stopped at the sight. She stopped in her tracks when she saw *him*, a handsome and charming young man who had traveled far from Corconia, the sister town of Marsonia, to explore the famous ghost town he had heard so much about. He hadn't expect to find a cabin in the middle of the dusty barren land, so when he did, he just had to stop.

"Hello, there, my name's Ashwell, Ashwell Ardelean. And you are?" the man introduced himself.

"Marietta, Marietta Covici," she replied.

Ashwell was tall, handsome, and the complete opposite of Lord Blackwell. They immediately fell in love and settled down at his home in Corconia, where they lived a prosperous and comfortable lifestyle, and he loved her with everything he had and promised to be by her side no matter what the curse was. It didn't take long before she married the greatest man of all time and became his faithful wife.

"My love, please, I love you dearly with all my heart. Please, will you do me the honor of being my wife, and together, we shall live in eternal happiness?" He popped the question less than three months later, and Marietta couldn't be happier.

It's what she had always wanted. She didn't care that Ashwell wasn't royalty. She didn't care that there was still a high chance the Queen Azra's army would come after her, find her, and kill her. She just wanted to start over, live the life she had always wanted before she ever met the royal family.

But still, she lived in fear.

Ashwell always dreamt of having children, fine with the fact that the child residing in Marietta's abdomen belonged to another man. But Marietta feared the fate of the curse, the fate her child would be born with. She had sworn off men after that night, and especially after Cross, but Ashwell felt too perfect for her to resist. The thought of losing a chance at happiness with someone who truly loved her and a chance to stop feeling so alone outweighed the thought of giving birth to a monster.

Which was why she could never drum up the courage to confess to him that she was an abnormal. Her secret had been the reason she lost both Lord Cross and Morgana, and Marietta knew that if she wanted to keep Ashwell by her side, she needed to hide her secret at all cost. She'd simply figure out a way to explain her child's strange ability when the time came. Perhaps she could even pin the responsibility on Lord Cross.

However, Ashwell's love for her soon made her forget about the curse and why she had been so afraid. He promised her that no matter what happened, he'd be by her side forever. If she had a boy, they'd name him Ashwell the second, after his father. If the child were a girl... well, they'd have to find a better name. She wanted the child to be nothing like her or Desdemona.

And to an extent, that became true. Because destiny had a curious way of working itself out.

Several months later, the day finally came, and their newborn child was a girl. The birth of her daughter was more painful than anything she had ever experienced before, lying on her back and pushing harder and harder until the child came out.

Aura, they had named her, with her transparent brown eyes and striking black hair, staring back at them. Marietta saw nothing wrong, just a sweet and innocent little girl with most beautiful of faces smiling back at her. She hugged the child and cried in joy, but Ashwell fainted from the shock of seeing his daughter. He must've seen something that Marietta wasn't able to, a shock so devastating that he was never the same again.

Ashwell spent the next several months constantly depressed and paralyzed, like he'd seen a ghost. He refused to eat, speak, or even sleep, simply lying awake every night until his eyes burned too much to carry on. He couldn't stand to look at the child, refusing to tend to her needs even as she cried. He didn't want to go anywhere near that... that creature, as he'd called her. He had once been such a joyous and happy man. Now, he was nothing but the hollow shell of a person. Marietta tried to help him, help him snap out of whatever he was going through and tell her what he'd seen, but nothing seemed to work. She couldn't help but blame herself for ruining his life. If they had never met, he'd probably still be full of life.

One morning, she found his body hanging from a tree.

Six

Twenty-Five Years Later

A man grabbed onto Aura's shoulder like she was part of his property. It was just too bad that he didn't know who, or what, she really was. This wasn't her first rendezvous. She had dealt with men like him before. Sure, they all found her hideous, her face almost a sin to look at, but regardless, they always fell for her charm, her essence that drove them toward a necessary evil. It had been this way ever since she was a child.

Aura never knew how others saw her. They all seemed to

run before she could find out. To her and her mother, she was beautiful, as gorgeous and radiant as the other beautiful ladies in Corconia. So, how come the men all ran away from her instead of toward her? How come women with half her beauty got all the attention while she received all the shame? She just didn't understand.

For the first fifteen years of her life, this tragedy pained her greatly. The confusion between what she was seeing and what everyone else was seeing drove her to a point of insanity. She would hide inside her home, refusing to let the world see her.

But that all changed on her sixteenth birthday. Being a second-generation half-vampire, her abilities only began to develop when she turned sixteen, and that excitement and thrill she felt from being so powerful instantly made her insecurities disappear. She now wanted to experience the world, see what the world outside her home had to offer and what she'd been missing out on all these years. Her mother allowed her to drink blood from the woodland creatures living behind their home, warning her that whenever she felt hungry, animal blood was all she could drink. Human blood was off-limits; Marietta had learned the hard way. She swore that she'd never go back, not after all the trouble it caused, and she made Aura promise that she never would either.

But as Aura grew older, the thirst grew stronger. The stench of human blood was much more potent than that of animals, and she couldn't stop craving it whenever she was near mortals.

And she tried to refrain. She tried to remain an obedient child, but she could only keep it up for so long.

As the years passed, the migraines and illness grew worse the more she withdrew. She could see her mother growing sicker and sicker, and Aura feared that she'd become like her soon enough. Finally, on her twentieth birthday, she caved. She gave into her cravings and drained her first human, a tacky-looking man who was walking his dog near her home. He was alone, so knew she'd be safe from anyone seeing her. And the blood! She didn't regret her decision at all, even if she had been caught. The warm blood tasted so delicious on her tongue that she imagined it was what Heaven felt like. She took her time, draining the man of everything he had, and then threw him in a trench. Her mother saw her, of course. She didn't hide it very well, or at all, in fact. And Aura promised that it was only a one-time thing, but both her and Marietta knew that once the taste of human blood touched a vampire's tongue, it can become very difficult to turn back.

And so, she didn't. For years, Aura would throw a cloak over her head and run out in search for her next prey. Her striking eyes were the only part of her face that men didn't run from. In fact, one look into them, and they usually found themselves instantly enticed. And that's how she was able to entrap so many of her feed. Her second kill happened in an alleyway beside the saloon she frequented often, where she knew single men who wouldn't be missed often visited. He was so drunk out of his mind that he barely even knew what was happening until he was as good as dead. Her third kill happened just one night apart. A beggar on the streets asked her for some pocket change when she lured him to his death instead, with a promise of gold coins he never did get. And all her victims were usually men. She didn't know why, but their blood always tasted much sweeter. She had tried drinking female blood once, but there was nothing satisfying about the thick and bitter liquid trickling down her throat. Never again would she go down that path.

She had the map of town engraved in her mind. It would be easy, so easy to just drag him into the woods and drain the life out of him. People could try to stop her, but that would only lead them to their own demise.

When he pulled down the hood of her cloak, she let out a

cackled laugh as he stumbled back in terror. Her eyes were the one thing she found that men didn't mind. Her beautiful eyes that lured them all in and gave them hope that they'd have yet another gullible peasant girl to warm their beds. But no, she was no ordinary girl.

When he regained his composure, he leaned in close again, mesmerized as the rest of the scarf fell off her face. He looked at her like she was deformed and scarred, and he felt entitled to take her, almost as if he was able to *because* she didn't represent the conventional standard of beauty.

But before he could, Aura took him first, leaning in to give him a kiss before digging her fangs into his neck. The rush of hunting the men in town, the pigs who thought they could treat women like objects, always made her feel better. It wasn't her fault that they cherished their erections more than they did their lives. It wasn't her fault that they all willingly chose to follow her into the dark abyss.

Their warm blood was something she simply could not refuse.

She rarely ever made the first move, giving them full control at first so they'd think they were in charge. It wasn't until they were both deep into the woods that he began to backtrack. He was visibly uncomfortable and seemed ready to bolt.

"What is it?" she asked.

"Nothing. I just—something hurt my neck," the man said.

He wasn't looking as brave now that the roles were reversed, was he?

Aura wanted to laugh. Instead, she kissed and caressed him, letting his hands wander. Men were always the same. They always wanted to take something, as if it belonged to them, even humans. And if they were turned down or rejected, they acted like giant babies.

It felt a little too intense at first. The first cut was certainly always the deepest, whether physically on them or emotionally on her. Grazing him tight, she whispered words of passion into his ear. The touch between them was fire, tearing off each other's clothes and biting each other softly until it all became too real. Once he caught a glimpse of her face again, the dark blood dripping from her lips, he screamed.

She laughed. She watched with glee as he ran away from her, hoping to escape between the convoluted trees. That never worked.

She played with him, gave him a head start, and then she followed him. It didn't take long before she caught up to him, sunk her teeth into his skin once again, and watched as the blood flowed down his naked body. Then she lowered her head and drank to her heart's content.

It tasted delicious.

Of fear and pain.

Of revenge.

Of justice.

"You could have treated me better. I actually kind of liked you at first," she teased.

"Y-You a-are a demon!" the man screamed, eyes bulging out with both terror and shock.

Such a shame, too. If only he wasn't such a pig, she could see them making a life together, having babies, the whole nine yards. It was a pity. She could picture him with a carriage and roses, a happily ever after. But no, her reality was far removed from that dream.

When she sank her teeth into his skin once more, he screamed louder, but there wasn't much of a fight left in him as she drank voraciously until everything left inside him was gone, then his body sagged and dropped to the ground.

She felt the blood flow through her, dripping from her fingertips.

It was truly such a pity.

If it wasn't for her ravenous desire and thirst for blood, maybe she could've finally found love, after all these years of searching. She always had difficulty finding someone who would stay, especially after she removed her mask. Her mother always told her she was the most beautiful child around, so how come no one else could see that? Must be the curse, the horrific curse brought about by her mother's selfishness. That only made her want to kill even more. To make everyone else suffer and remain alone like she was.

After burying the body deep beneath the dirt, Aura trudged home, climbed into bed, and lied there motionless until the silent night calmed her mind.

HER MOTHER HAD WARNED HER TO STOP DRINKING blood. After Marietta almost got killed and the consequence Aura had to live with her entire life, Aura vowed to swear it off completely, a promise she made years ago that she had failed to keep time and time again. Such a fool she had been as a child. She didn't realize how delicious the warm liquid would feel coursing down her throat.

For nearly five years, she had kept her promise, hunting and killing only the small animals behind her home. But then the rage intensified from the mockery and rejection she faced, and the hunger became much, much stronger. Marietta had been able to withstand the urge, but then again, all of this was her fault, and the guilt rode in her for decades.

Aura even tried imprisoning herself, entrapping her own free will away from temptation, but yet, she still found her mouth around another man's neck every other night.

But that didn't mean she didn't try to stop. She did, many times. The horrid cries and hateful chants of the dead running through her mind, however, were all too strong for her to remain calm, letting her anxiety take over her body.

They hated her; all her ghosts did. And so did she.

But that was her curse.

Now that she could finally understand it, her mother was right.

The property, which Marietta had easily acquired before Aura was born, was largely the same as the first day they moved in after her father died. The building was built in black stone, and it was framed with statues of angels. The windows were dark and let very little sunlight in, and its appearance was as sinister as that of Castle Vesunna.

Her mother relished in this, the fact that the two of them would have the entire home to themselves. But Aura thought that was all just meaningless. Much like life itself, everyone just pretended to care about things, when in reality, no one realized that the only guarantee life brought with it was despair.

Marietta continued her joy by bragging about how she was able to charm the town of Corconia into sparing their home from the mass demolishment, a thought that made Aura's stomach churn. Her mother, with beauty that never seemed to age, had always been able to attract suitors. Her face glowed with the sunlight, while Aura was usually stuck with the disgusting older men who only wanted her because she was young and naïve.

However, by a strange coincidence, all those men involved in the demolition had gone missing near the woods or died several months later, as if something, or someone, had sucked the life out of them.

Aura knew the truth. That it was Marietta who had done it.

But it wasn't until several years later that her mother began to realize how awful it all was, the act she had done.

The circumstances of these tragedies were mysterious, and

a reputation struck the domain. No one ever came near the cursed home again, or at least, the smart ones didn't. And that gave them room to do whatever they wanted. But that only made Aura feel angrier and lonelier, stuck as a prisoner inside her own home, a curse within a curse. She hated her mother for what she had done. Because of her, she could never venture out during the day for fear of someone recognizing her as the daughter of the monster.

Aura kicked the walls, the echoes of her own movement mocking her. She hated her life. Hated everyone. Wanted them all dead. But there was nothing Aura despised more than herself. The way she looked on the outside... the way she felt on the inside. It was all the same. Dark and dark. Blood and sinning. And she would never escape it.

Madness seemed to run in the family.

Sometimes, she would hear Marietta speak about her own mother, Desdemona, Aura's grandmother. She always looked so sad when she did it, leaving Aura to wonder if she was also an unwanted child. After all, her mother only cared about secrets, and when she thought Aura wasn't looking, she glanced at her with pity. Or perhaps, she felt just as lonely as Aura did.

A knock on the door took her out of her grim mood.

"Who is it?" she called out.

"Who else would it be? Let me in."

Seven

Aura stepped aside to let her mother walk through the door, looking right at home with her disheveled hair and torn nightgown, just another day in the life of Marietta Covici. Her eyes were bloodshot, and her fangs were showing through her twisted smile.

"My dear daughter," she said.

"Mother," Aura answered. "How are you?"

"Not too bad," her mother replied. She looked like she hadn't fed in months.

"If I were you, I'd stay away from me. I reek of blood," Aura warned. "I didn't get a chance to clean myself up yet."

"I will only bother you for a moment, dear," Marietta responded. "I need you to do something for me."

"What is it?" she asked.

"Herbs," her mother replied. "I need you to help me get these herbs... Rumor has it that it's good for withdrawal."

Aura didn't say anything else. There was no point in saying anything else. Night after night, all their conversations were the same, the same empty and shallow small talk that would last less than two minutes, and ending with her mother asking for a favor.

Aura sighed and extended her hand, and her mother gave her the yellow leaflet.

"Find Ophelia, in the heart of the city. She'll know what's needed," Marietta said. "And hurry, before I get worse."

"Mother, I thought our people didn't become ill?"

"They do after drinking only animal blood for an extended period of time... that wretched Azra. If it wasn't for her, I wouldn't be so afraid."

With no other choice, Aura grabbed her cloak and pulled the hood over her face.

Her mother continued to stare off to the side of Aura's face. Even when she was helping her, Aura knew that Marietta couldn't stand to look at her daughter without feeling guilt and an uncontrollable thirst for blood.

Shaking her head, Aura grabbed her scarf off the railing and guarded her face as she always did. Even at night, there was still a high chance of someone noticing her, or worse, being scared off by her.

She opened the door and walked out into the chilly night, the snowy wind blowing at her as she tried to push through.

Everybody knew their cozy little town wasn't a friendly place, let alone one where she could find the love of her life.

When she got to the gates of the city, she saw a man standing by the alley. He wasn't as tall as the last one, and she was still full, but the way he smiled at her, so charming, that she definitely found herself interested. But she couldn't give into her hunger, not yet, anyway. She had a mission. Her mother was waiting.

She descended further down the dark streets, where she soon found an old woman selling the same herb her mother had requested. She was short and petite, dressed in a dark violet cloak and holding a wooden cane shaped like a serpent. She seemed awfully mysterious, shady even, and Aura hesitated at first before approaching her.

"Are you Ophelia?" Aura asked as she stepped up.

The old woman was not easy on the eyes. Her large warts and violet eyes were dead giveaways that there was indeed something supernatural about her.

"That's the name. What do you want?" the woman asked aggressively.

Aura simply held up the leaf after taking a deep breath, before handing over the small bag of coins her mother had given her.

"Marietta, Marietta, Marietta," Ophelia chanted. She opened the bag, and an instant frown fell on her face. "Just twenty? Where's the rest?"

"Be thankful I brought any money at all," Aura retorted. "She isn't getting any better. I'm starting to think whatever you're giving her is only making her worse."

Suddenly, a gust of wind brought the scent of fresh cider and a touch of cologne to Aura's nose. She turned around and saw a man watching her, the same man she had seen beside the alley.

Is he following me? She thought to herself.

She stared back.

"Who is that man?" she turned to ask Ophelia.

The woman cackled. Then shook her head.

"Blade Cross. Stay away from him. He is twice as deadly as all my potions combined, and that would be a slow and painful death. Mine, at least, kills you on the spot."

"But he seems so regal, so elegant. He must be of higher quality than all the other men."

"Don't make that mistake. I have seen your entire family, generation after generation, falling for terrible men like him. Besides, he *is* the reason why you have such an ug—uncanny beauty. Your mother told me all about it."

"Him? He's the reason for this curse? How do you know?" Aura touched her face. Her skin did feel ugly. Why couldn't she see it?

"He carries the crest of his family. Look at him." Ophelia pointed at his lapel.

She was right. Although God had cursed her with ugliness and loneliness, at least her senses had been left untouched.

And from where she was, she could see the way his green crest complimented his green eyes and long black hair.

She looked back at the old woman one more time, who handed her a big stack of herbs in a basket.

"Whatever you do, give this to your mother before the sun rises. And remember, stay away from Blade Cross. He will do nothing but ruin you, just like his father."

Father? Ignoring the warning, Aura did just the opposite, walking straight toward the stunningly handsome man instead.

When she knocked into him, she made it seem like an accident. But it wasn't. Her vision was way above average, and her senses could tell where she was going even before her eyes could. She had to find out if what the old woman said was true, see who this man really was and whether he *was* the key to finally breaking her curse. Living under an old rag was growing more and more tiring by the day. People were scared of her, for the reason she didn't want them to be.

"Oops, sorry," she muttered when their bodies collided, pulling her scarf up to shield the bottom of her face even more.

As the man known as Blade apologized, she could smell the scent of fresh lemon and mint coming off him. Seeing the perch of his nose and the way his lips moved as he talked, she was already feeling the need to drink his blood. It had been hours since her last feed, and she was beginning to feel the lightheadedness.

I bet he tastes like sweet candy, she thought. *Lemon and strawberry, flavors I can never resist.*

"Sorry, miss. I should really watch where I'm going. Are you alright? Have I injured you?" he asked, staring into her eyes with worry. His eyes were deep and enchanting, and she didn't notice herself staring for much longer than appropriate until he asked again. "Miss, are you alright?"

He didn't seem like the monster the elderly woman had painted him out to be. Maybe he wasn't like the rest of his family after all.

"I'm fine," Aura answered. "Just a little scattered, that's all. I'm glad you were here to catch me. A true knight in shining armor." She winked at him.

He stared at her with affection, looking at her as if she were a beautiful flower. She could smell the fresh blood running through his veins, pulsating and ripe for her taking. He then asked her if she needed any help carrying the basket of herbs back home as she continued to hide her face, covered by her scarf and veil. Aura saw the way his eyes moved across her face with curiosity, but instead of inserting himself into her personal space, he seemed as taken aback by her as she was by him.

Once again, the dark impulse to take him then and there

overcame her. She wanted to bite down on his lips and splash his blood all over the streets, taking him hard. She was so hungry that she couldn't care less where she was or who was watching. She wanted him. No, she needed him.

Suddenly, someone coughed behind them. She turned her head slightly, and with the corner of her eye, saw a thin man with dark red hair and a pointed nose who had come up behind Blade.

"Lord Blade. Have you finished with your purchases for today? We need you to come home with us back to Luceria. Now. Your father says it's urgent!"

Blade turned to face Aura, letting her go from his grip. "Are you sure you're okay, miss…?" he asked.

"Aura. Aura Ardelean." She smiled and nodded her head, forgetting that he couldn't even see the lower half of her face.

"Well, Miss Aura. Such a pretty name. I am glad that you are alright. My name is Blade. Blade Cross."

The man behind him coughed again, his impatience noticeably frustrating Blade. He turned to him. "Just give me a minute, okay, Florin? I'm in the middle of something."

"Understood. I'll let you two finish up," Florin responded.

As promised, he left them alone, though glancing over at Aura a couple of times as if she was up to something devilish. Her dark veil must have scared him. But she didn't care; she only had eyes for Blade.

And Blade seemed just as enchanted by her as he couldn't stop looking into her mesmerizing eyes. Although he was sure enough not interested in her beauty, he looked puzzled by her, like he was drawn to something. She could feel the weight of his stare on her. Men always felt drawn to her energy. She guessed it was another side effect of the curse.

Ah, yes, men were always curious, but once they saw her face, all affections would simply vanish.

Some of them, the ones who liked to pretend they were

gentlemen and not barbaric, would usually try to offer her something to drink, and when they got her drunk enough, they would try to lure her away, hoping she would service them for the night.

And that's when she would kill them.

Aura continue to look at Blade, cautious as to whether or not he would try and do the same. She almost wished he wouldn't. Her face warmed from his touch, but then she remembered that her sick mother was still at home waiting for her.

"I... I have to go," she muttered and began heading off in the opposite direction.

"Wait!" Blade shouted, grabbing hold of her arm.

"Yes?" she responded, part of her fearing that Blade had already figured out who she was.

"You seem familiar, like I know you somehow. I just can't pinpoint it."

"No, we don't know each other. Look, I'm sorry, but I really have to go. My mother is waiting for me."

However, as she turned to leave, her scarf caught around his fingers and fell off her face, exposing the face that always succeeded in scaring people away. She felt so exposed, so vulnerable. And her anxiety only skyrocketed when he gasped.

"I'm a monster!" Aura wailed and ran away.

I knew it, Aura thought as she climbed up the stairs to give her mother the basket of herbs. *They're all the same. Each and every single one of them, disgusting.*

"Aura, honey," Marietta said with labored breaths when she saw her. "You look like you just saw a ghost." She took a vial out from the basket and poured it down her throat.

Aura removed her cloak and walked over to the window to stare out at the full moon and then back at her mother. Even in the darkness of the room and near death, Marietta still remained beautiful, and Aura resented that she could never be like that, that she would be alone forever because of her selfish mother.

"I didn't," she replied.

Marietta coughed a fit of blood.

"You need to drink blood, Mother. Human blood," Aura said, wrapping a cotton blanket around her shoulders. "You can't keep going like this. You'll end up dead sooner than you know it."

"You know I can't do that, not anymore," Marietta answered. "If Queen Azra ever finds out that I drained another human, she'd have my head for sure." She stopped to cough again on her handkerchief, blood dripping off the side of her hand.

"But Mother, we're no longer in Marsonia. Queen Astra has no power over you anymore. She can't control you!"

"Azra, honey, Queen Azra." Marietta corrected her. "Still, she has eyes everywhere. She's not like the rest of them, Aura. She's an abnormal, an extremely powerful abnormal. Trust me, she'll know."

Aura punched the wall. It was unbecoming of a lady, but she had never been much of a lady. "What's the difference if you're going to die like this anyway?"

Marietta lowered her head. "I feel like I'm already dead. The day Queen Azra cursed me. I feel like I'm already dead."

"Cursed? You?" Aura really began fuming now. "Queen Azra cursed you? I'm the hideous one! Do you know how many men run from me like I'm some kind of monster when they see me? And the worst part is, I don't even know what they're running from. I don't even know where to begin changing myself to stop them from running. I'm the one who has to live with this curse, not you! If you want to die so badly, just jump off the tower then instead of feeling sorry for yourself all the time. We'll both be in hell soon enough anyway."

She didn't wait for her mother to answer before storming out of the room and slamming the door behind her.

Aura found herself deep in thought the next morning. If her mother wasn't willing to stand up for herself and reclaim her legacy, she would. She was tired of those far inferior to her dictating how she should live her life, long before she was even born. It made her even angrier knowing that one of those people was her own mother.

She got up and looked around. Marietta was still in bed. She usually slept until the afternoon. If Aura was going to act, she had to do it now. If she could sneak out without her mother waking up, maybe she could find Lord Blade before he left Corconia. It was a highly unlikely chance, but she could still hope. And maybe, she could get some answers out of him and find out how to break the curse. After all, he *was* of Lucerian royalty. He had to know *something*.

She didn't care that there was a higher chance of getting caught out in the daylight. She didn't care that there was a chance that she'd be killed. She just wanted to be done with this curse once and for all.

If he didn't comply, well, things would only end badly for him. She would have her revenge either way, and he would meet his death. It would all be poetic. The same way her grandfather was killed. She would be willing to die to avenge her legacy.

Her mother wouldn't agree. But fortunately, she was still recovering from the lack of blood in her system, and when she went out, she remained immobile.

Ophelia was nowhere in sight when Aura arrived through the gates. Perhaps she knew what was about to unfold and didn't want to get caught in the middle of it.

Her prayers were answered. When she got to the town square, Blade Cross was there, speaking with a shop owner who stood in front of a trinket stand.

Aura tried to remain discreet, to conceal the fact that she'd been searching for him. Quietly, she tried to sneak past behind him, hoping to duck around the adjacent fruit stand so she could eavesdrop on his conversation.

However, her plan didn't go as expected. Instead, she tripped on her cloak and knocked herself into the fruit stand, sending oranges and apples alike flying through the air as the merchant tried to keep himself from falling over.

"What are you? Blind? Watch where you're stepping! You better pay me back for everything you destroyed. That's a whole day's income!" The merchant was flustered, his nose scrunched, and wrinkles forming on his forehead.

"So... sorry, sir," Aura tried to apologize, but her words were not enough to feed his family.

And that's when Blade walked over. With every step, Aura's dead heart beat faster and faster... and she felt her emotions clash as she saw his beautiful eyes shine with intensity while his hands combed through his beautiful long hair.

He walked up to the merchant. "I'm terribly sorry, sir. Please excuse my friend here. I'm sure it was just an accident." He reached into his pocket, pulled out a bag of gold coins, and handed it to him. "Here, this should pay for everything that was ruined."

Friend? He thinks of me as his friend?

Still infuriated, the merchant snatched the bag out from his hand and counted. "Alright, you're off the hook this time, but young lady, if I ever see you around my shop again, you won't be so lucky." He pointed at Aura before proceeding to pick up his dented fruit, shaking his head and muttering in a language she couldn't understand.

When Blade led her away, she quickly turned to him and curtsied. "Thank you, Sir Blade. Thank you for helping me."

He grinned. "Actually, I'm glad that I was able to find you here. Otherwise, I would've searched all over town. My father summoned me home last night, but I knew I couldn't leave without finding you and apologizing to you first. I'm incredibly sorry for being so rude to you yesterday. I apologize sincerely for my reaction."

That disarmed her. She stood there in silence for a moment, unsure of how to answer.

"I'm sorry about my behavior. I didn't mean to hurt you. I was...," he continued, inching closer to her.

"Taken aback by my deformity?" she finally said. "Everybody does—"

"It isn't a deformity," he interrupted.

"What is it then, if not a deformity?" she demanded.

People were already staring at them. Even with the long scarf covering her face and neck, she could see how people watched their verbal sparring, how they stared at her in confusion for wearing such a thick cloak under the beating sun.

"I-I don't know," Blade admitted, then composed himself. "But being rude and scared shouldn't be the automatic response to your condition..."

Condition? I'll let him see how truly hideous I am. I'll let them all see, she thought and removed her scarf and hood.

The townspeople gathered around them, pointing and ridiculing her appearance. She cried out tears of anger instead of pain, but she let them all believe it was of sadness.

"This is your family's doing, you know," she said. "Do you want to know the true reason why I'm so hideous? Ask your father about Marietta and the curse that befell upon her, and how he did nothing but hurt her and betrayed her." She spun around on her heel. "Now, if you'll excuse me, I need to get back home to my mother. She needs me!"

And so, she turned her back on the man, who was rendered speechless after her little outburst. Her plan worked. Not a moment after, she found him grabbing her arm.

It disgusted her. The way he thought pitying her was enough to win her over.

"Don't touch me," she said as she pulled back.

He released her, but the look of sadness in his eyes almost made her feel sorry for him.

"Is that true? Did my family hurt you?" he asked.

"You'll have to find out yourself. Go, and ask him. Tell him how the life of a little girl was tragically ruined because he was so desperate to become king that he didn't stop Queen Azra. Tell him about my monstrosity. Then come and meet me here after midnight. I want to know what he says. I want him to admit what they did to us... what they did to me. Until then, I have nothing left to say to you."

She wrapped her face with the scarf again.

"Wait!" he screamed, then lowered the tone of his voice. "Don't go, please. Whatever it is he did to you... I apologize on his behalf. My father didn't used to behave like this. He used to be one of the kindest men in the kingdom. But after Lord Blackwell died, I don't know, all the power just went straight to his head. I'm sure he acted out of grief rather than malice."

Aura smiled underneath her scarf. Blade didn't noticed. He seemed to be coping with the tale she had just told him. A tale that was as true as it was twisted.

After all, her mother *did* kill the man's brother. But Blade, being as noble as he was, couldn't very well know that.

"Please, tell me more about that night. I want to know what really happened," he continued. His eyes were imploring.

"Ask him," Aura said before pushing him away with all her strength.

It was clear, by the way that he fell to the ground like a

ragdoll thrown by a wild child, that he wasn't expecting her to be so strong.

Even after knowing the truth, he was underestimating her, and that enraged her.

Aura ran away and hid in the nearest alleyway. Nothing had changed. People were just as clueless as they had been earlier, and she was just as sad as she had always been, but now, she'd started the spark of doubt in Blade's heart and the undoing of his family.

She would have her revenge soon.

Eight

The stress from her interaction with Blade triggered her thirst for blood. She could've just taken him, drained him, and that would be her ultimate revenge. But she couldn't. He was just so captivating that she couldn't bear to end his life. But that didn't mean that she couldn't end his father's life.

Though, she couldn't do anything on an empty stomach. She was ravenous, hiding in the woods and sniffing out the perfect bait until it turned dark enough to spring into action. It didn't take long before she found him. Tall, blonde, and slim. No wedding band. The collar of his overcoat popped up, and enough cologne on his neck and gel in his hair that he smelled like he just walked out of a beauty magazine.

Aura wrinkled her nose, trying to push past the awful smell of old spice and cedarwood, and focus on the saccharine blood coursing through his veins. It was a challenge, but she managed to suppress her repulsion when he walked in front of her.

"Hey, there," Aura teased as she popped out from behind the trees. "I haven't seen you around these blocks lately." She had fashioned her scarf back together, but strands of her wavy hair fell loose over her shoulders. She curled the strands around her finger. She felt so ugly on the inside. That's what others had led her to believe, but that didn't stop her from pretending to be beautiful and seductive.

The man stopped walking, drawn to Aura by her enchanting eyes. He smirked, combed his hair with his fingers, and headed toward her way.

It was working, the closer he got, the more her mouth salivated. She could almost smell what his blood would taste like, and she was hungry!

"Well, hello, there," he said, reaching for her right hand and bringing it to his mouth to kiss the back of it. "What's a pretty girl like you doing all alone here at night? Best be careful. There are a lot of delinquents around this part of town who would have no problem taking advantage of you."

"Oh?" Aura asked, pretending to be surprised. "Is that so? You mean delinquents like you? Is that why you're here? To search for and take advantage of pretty girls?"

He chuckled. "Now, I see why you would think that, but no, darling. I am a perfect gentleman." He reached out a hand. "Name's Xavier."

She had no interest in shaking his hand but did so anyway.

She couldn't send out red flags that fast; it would only scare him away. "Elizabeth," she said.

She never used her true identity around her victims. Although she had been lucky enough that all the men she fed on ended up perishing, she always feared that one would get away and expose her. Like Marsonia, Corconia wasn't accepting of abnormals. Just last year, they burned a woman because they thought she was a witch. Turned out, she was just psychotic with hallucinations. But if they were willing to treat someone so innocent so badly, she couldn't imagine what they would do to her if they found out she was a vampire.

"Elizabeth, I'm quite fond of that name." Xavier rubbed his fingers on his chin. "Such a regal name. Wait, don't tell me you're royalty."

Aura shook her head. "Nope, just your average peasant girl looking for a good time."

"Good time, you say. Well, how about I take you back to my place and show you a good time?"

"I would love to, but I don't want to be a bother. I'm sure you have people you live with who wouldn't want an intruder coming into their home."

He took the bait. "Nah, you don't have to worry about that. I live alone. Just a single bachelor hoping for some company and someone to hold on this chilly night." He moved closer to her and touched the part of her scarf that covered her left cheek. "You look so beautiful, Elizabeth. I bet you're even more gorgeous behind all that fabric you're hiding under. Come, let me take you back to my place. I will show you how a true gentleman treats a lady."

She didn't say another word and followed him. A fifteen-minute walk from where they were took them back to a quaint neighborhood where homes were each a hundred feet apart.

That should be far enough where no one can hear us. Aura

carefully planned out her actions in her head. He made it way too easy for her, inviting her into his home like this. She didn't even have to put up a fight.

When they walked in through the front door, the stench in his home was even worse than the stench on his body. Garbage littered the floor, stains painted the walls, and although she couldn't see it, she swore there was a dead carcass lying around somewhere.

But he didn't seem to mind, plopping himself down on the couch and gesturing for her to join him. Aura had wanted to take it slow, ease him in and prime his blood for her taking, but she couldn't stand the smell. She just wanted this to be done and over with.

Sitting down next to him, she began to rub his leg.

"Ooo, feisty and straight to the point. I like it," he flirted.

Then he reached over and began to undo her scarf. Aura's body tensed, preparing herself for his reaction.

And just as she thought, he quickly backed away, falling onto the floor and grabbing his umbrella, holding it between them. This made Aura think about Blade, how he also saw her face, but unlike the others, he didn't run.

Unlike this guy. As he threw the umbrella at her and bolted to the front door, she swiftly ran up to him and grabbed him by the shoulders, her strength tossing him straight across the living space.

"D-Don't kill me, please. I won't tell anyone, I promise!"

Aura removed her hood and took off her cloak, her full face in view for the man to see. She peered up at the mirror above from where he was sitting and looked at her own reflection, but she still couldn't see what everyone else had been so terrified of. Her nose wasn't gargantuan, her cheeks weren't sunken in, and her skin was definitely not peeling or shedding.

I just don't understand.

Looking down at the man, who was now sweating bullets

and wetting himself, she leaned down to his level and kissed him on the lips. "Sweet Xavier, sweet, sweet Xavier. Why would I kill you? We're here to have fun, remember?"

Then she kissed him again, her lips so tantalizing that she found him kissing back, just like they all do. She led his lips down to her neck, stripping off her own clothes and allowing him to explore her body. She then stripped him down, and they began to make love.

Just then, a piercing cry came out of his mouth. He glanced down and found her fangs digging into his right shoulder, sinking in deeper and deeper and refusing to unleash. He screamed again, trying to fight her off, but she was much too strong for him. His last scream barely made it out of his mouth as she bit down on his lips and ripped them off in one fell swoop. About a minute later, he was gone, lying on the floor as nothing but the skin and bones of what used to be a human. Poor thing, he never got the chance to feel like a man.

WHEN SHE ARRIVED BACK HOME, SHE LET GO OF ALL the layers of clothing covering her. Then she went to check on her mother. Aura saw her mother's labored breathing, and all the anger she had felt toward her just disintegrated. She seemed so weak...

"Mother!" she cried, after wetting a rag and dabbing it onto her face with the most utmost care.

Her mother's eyes opened. For a moment, she was calm, then it all changed. She pursed her lips, and her death glare was enough of an indication to how she felt.

"Aura."

Her mother's welcoming wasn't warm at all. Her spirit seemed as crushed as they were whenever they fought.

"Are you alright, Mother?" Aura asked with a voice so thin that sounded foreign to her own ears.

"Tell me you have some good news after such a long stroll," her mother said spitefully.

"I have news, whether it's good or not is up to you. I'm sure that you would love to hear what, no, who I found out there."

Her mother seemed sad, the expression on her face dropping.

"I had a dream... of you and I running away. We were happy and healthy. We were rich." Marietta coughed, words rasping through her vocal chords with impetus. "I wish I hadn't woken up. If what you have for me is bad news, save it. I'd rather lie in bed and wait until my body can't help but stop functioning."

Aura held onto her mother's hands. Her eyes and throat itched.

"I have found the way back to our dream life," Aura said.

"How?" her mother asked.

"I met someone, someone with a name you will surely find familiar."

Her mother's face blanched. Her touch on Aura's hands stung.

"Don't do anything we'll both regret later, Aura," her mother warned. "It's never a good idea to revisit the past, especially if the past had brought nothing but pain."

"You won't regret it, Mother. I promise. The man I met... he might change our destiny. Forever."

"Who—?"

"His name is Blade Cross. Does that sound familiar to you?" Aura asked.

Marietta swallowed. Her eyes turned wide open, and she looked like she was having a fever, with her reddened cheeks and hot hands.

"No, it can't be. Could it be that he's Lord Cross' son?" Marietta nearly fainted, as if all the memories of her past just rushed back to her. "He... he found someone else... got intimate... had a child." Then she grabbed the vase beside her and threw it against the window in her room, smashing it into smithereens and creating a sizable crack on the glass. "That was supposed to be me!" she shouted.

Aura shrunk back. She didn't know the full story between Lord Cross and her mother. But she did know the reason for her mother's eternal antagonism toward him: she loved him, and he betrayed her.

"According to Ophelia, yes, Blade is Lord Cross' son," Aura replied. "I've met him twice now. But Mother, I really think he can help us. I really think he's the key to finally breaking this curse."

Marietta shook her head.

"Whatever it is you're planning... You have to know that he's dangerous. All of them are."

Aura laughed. "You don't have to fear them," she said. "They, on the other hand... well, they have a lot to fear of us. Because I am as deadly as anyone can imagine."

"A-Aura! You don't know how dangerous they are. Especially Queen Azra. It is impossible to defeat her!" Marietta repeated, this time, trembling.

Aura touched her cheeks reflexively. An ornate mirror was hanging on the wall, far enough for her not to be able to see her reflection but close enough to remind her of how horrendous she appeared.

"Easy, Mother," Aura said, soothing her. "They won't be able to find us, not unless we want them to. I have spoken to him. He seems nice... almost too nice. Too gullible, just the way I like it."

"What did you do, Aura?" her mother demanded.

"I told him the truth. That they're all monsters... that they made me this way. You should have seen the way his noble face fell. He is naïve and trusting. Soon enough, we will have him at the palm of our hands. Soon, he will tell us the secret to breaking the curse… before leading us to *kill* his own family."

That brought some joy to her mother, and soon, she was smiling again. Aura couldn't believe it when Marietta hugged her.

"We will make them pay."

It was a pity that her mother's words would be followed by a cry of pain and her collapsing onto the bed.

Aura's arms felt like they were about to break off. Sure, she was strong, but her mother's body felt like the weight of a hundred bears. She didn't look it, but she definitely felt like it.

She was standing in the dark forest that crossed between Corconia and Marsonia, with her mother in her arms. Wolves passed by them, and Aura watched as her mother's chest rose and fell slowly.

She had fed her blood from one of the wolves to try and revive Marietta from her illness, and the animal's carcass was lying near them, drained and mangled. She tried to feel sad for killing the innocent wolf, but it had been a long time since she last cared about the wellbeing of another creature.

To Aura, everything was all about survival.

She let her mother rest on top of some dead leaves while she searched for another prey. It seemed like the death of that one animal had alerted the other animals to stay far, far away.

Aura let out a loud groan in frustration and kicked hard against a tree. Yellow and orange leaves fell on top of her, onto her hair, hood, and shoes. She dusted them off and stopped when she heard the sound of steps coming near her.

She cursed under her breath and picked her mother up again. Then she hid behind a tall pine tree and crouched behind its twigs. The sun had set, and traces of shadows were beginning to disappear. No one would see them. She had left her cloak at home, thinking the darkness of the night would conceal her appearance for long enough until she was able to save her mother.

The sound of boisterous laughter came closer, and so did the steps. It was then that she remembered that the old tavern, just a few yards away, would soon be opening up.

She held her breath while placing a hand over her mother's mouth and listened.

"I wish I had a woman to take care of me," said one of the men.

Another one answered, "I want someone loving, attractive, smart. The touch of a warm body, ready to take me—"

"Shh. Someone might hear us!" the first man interrupted.

Their steps were growing even closer.

She could smell them now. They stunk of sweat, alcohol, and other unsavory things, but their blood smelled delicious. It smelled like a warm supper, the entire family coming together at the dinner table and slicing into a juicy pot roast for everyone to enjoy, an experience she had only seen through the windows of others. It was something she would never get to enjoy.

But their blood would only be temporary. Soon, Aura would need to find others to keep her mother going, but this was good enough to keep her in decent health for the time being. Her mother would need to feed from them.

Another set of steps echoed throughout the forest. She looked around, expecting to find more incoming men, but the rustling of leaves gave way to a horse instead.

The mare went up in her hooves and ran away as she saw Aura approach, almost as if she knew.

Aura laughed. "Oh, Mother, the things I would do for you... I wouldn't do them for anyone else," she whispered to herself.

The steps soon stopped.

Then one of the bushes in front of them gave way to the two men. One was tall and skinny with a long nose and freckles; the other one was shorter and had a bald head, in spite of him looking the same age as Aura.

The two men looked at her with matching expressions of surprise. Then the taller one spoke, "Well, well, what do we have here? A young damsel and her mother in need of help? I guess it's a good thing we found you then."

Luckily, the shorter one had more common sense. He placed himself between his fool of a friend and the two women.

"Terrence, leave them alone. I'm sure they have enough to worry about without you harassing them," he countered.

The moon had now shifted, and the light was reflecting upon them. The forest wasn't in the shadows anymore, and Aura's scars were beginning to shine through.

Terrence's jaw quickly dropped upon seeing her face, even more so when he turned his gaze toward her mouth. It didn't take long for Aura to notice that her fangs were showing, the sharpness dangling in between her lips and sparkling in the moonlight.

It was now or never. She had to get to them before they got to her. She jumped to where they were and attacked Terrence. A blow to the head with her strength; then she twisted his head until she heard a loud snap. He went down quicker than she expected. He didn't even have a chance to plead for his life.

His friend was next. She had to chase him around the forest for a while, his stubby little legs much quicker than she'd thought, and he screamed the entire time. He cursed and tried to spit at her, but she stopped him by twisting his arms behind his back and immobilizing him, grabbing him before anyone heard.

The man cried out. He called her a demon. A witch. A monster. Nothing she hadn't heard before.

She laughed again.

"No, I'm not any of those, but I *am* going to kill you," she exclaimed. And then twisted his neck, too.

She carried Marietta to the shorter one and helped her drink until she regained consciousness. Then Aura walked over to Terrence, bent down, and sucked the remaining essence out of him.

Judging by how large the forest was, she imagined there was no chance that anyone would see them, even if there was a pub nearby. But she did have to cross a path on the way home, a path aligned with dozens of homes, with people who could come out at any minute and question the blood stains on them both.

Luckily, as they emerged from the woods and made the trip back to their own home, all the lights were still out, and everyone was asleep. No one suspected what had happened. No one even heard a thing. She wiped her mother's mouth with one of her sleeves and then her own, and they climbed up the steps together to get some rest.

THE FOLLOWING MORNING, HER MOTHER WAS IN better spirits. For once, she had rosy cheeks and a smile that changed her features to that of an innocent girl's.

"I told you drinking human blood was the only option, Mother," Aura exclaimed.

She walked over to the pile of bloody garments. She would

take them out back later that night and incinerate all the evidence. No one would ever find out.

"I was just so fearful of what Azra might do to me if she found out about this... I didn't think it would end well for either of us," Marietta defended herself.

"The queen only cursed me. You are exempt from any consequences, as far as I can see," Aura retorted in resentment.

The space between them seemed to shrink as they spoke. Aura felt herself suffocating from the stuffed air once again. She had saved her mother. Saved her! And she was *still* playing the victim. She needed to be somewhere else, anywhere else.

Aura wished she had a place to be. A home. Because there with her mother, she felt like she didn't belong, a stranger living under the roof of a drama queen.

"I truly regret what happened to you," Marietta apologized. Her mother came up to her. She touched her shoulder. "Îmi pare rău, fiica mea. I'm sorry. I promise to be there for you and finally break this curse. You can trust me," Marietta said.

Aura nodded. Then turned her glance onto her mother.

"Good, because I need your help."

A FEW DAYS LATER, MARIETTA WAS IN A MUCH better place than Aura had seen her in years. She was also happier, more vibrant, and energetic. Aura told her mother how Blade had reacted after seeing her face. She explained how he apologized and seemed genuinely sorry.

"He's not like the others, Mamă. He's... different. He doesn't run when he sees me, not like all the others. And I don't know why, but something tells me that he's used to looking at people like me."

Her mother looked pensive. She paced back and forth inside the room. Then she sat still for a moment.

Aura continued, telling Marietta about how she planned on ending Blade's life as revenge for what his family did to her if he didn't comply with her demands. However, Marietta disagreed. To her, Blade seemed like he had good intentions.

"I don't know, Aura. Someone who doesn't run away from you must really trust you."

Aura crossed her arms in front of her chest. "He pities me. That's all."

Her mother then touched her face with tenderness. "Fiica mea frumoasă, he won't pity you once he finds out what you're planning. But I trust your judgment. I'll help you. It's the least I can do."

Aura wasn't sure what to think. She feared that the men of Castle Vesunna would kill them both if they even stepped within a hundred feet of their property. And they couldn't take down the entire Lucerian army; there were too many of them.

Later that day, everything felt calm. The rift between the mother and daughter pair had somehow stopped, like all the effort they put mistrusting each other had been lifted off her shoulders. Aura thought about how to bring Blade closer to her. Now that her mother was better, all she had to focus on was revenge.

She had thought about just sinking her teeth into him and turning Blade into a vampire, a monster, just like her. What better way to seek revenge on Lord Cross than to have his own son murder him. It couldn't get any tastier than that. But that idea just didn't sit right with her. Turning someone else into what she was only created disgust and discomfort in her. Turning someone else into another weapon of destruction also wouldn't help her break her curse. She continued to ponder as she entered town through the passageway she had always used.

It was late enough in the evening, enough to avoid prying eyes. The perfect time to be there. She just needed some fresh air, somewhere she could be alone and reflect on everything that was going on around her. The evenings were always a safe time for her to simply walk around without being bothered. And even if she was, the dusk made it easy to dispose of any bodies.

When she arrived at the end of the alley, she felt better. The way the breeze touched her face even without her having to stand beneath the trees made her feel much calmer and at peace with herself.

That was until she thought about how lonely she was and that she probably always would be lonely.

Her curse made her feel isolated from the world. Disconnected. Wherever she went, everyone else had someone to be with. She didn't. She had no friends, no partner. It was just her and her mother. And even then, she felt unwanted. The loneliness was overwhelming, and taking someone else as a prisoner would probably solve nothing.

And the way Blade had behaved toward her made everything worse. Looking at him was like being adrift. Having to betray him and turn on him didn't sit well with her, either. But it was all she had. So, she swallowed hard, took her feelings, and hid them somewhere deep within her, along with her humanity.

Suddenly, she felt a hand on her shoulder.

When she spun around, there he was. With those same innocent eyes and that same expression of concern.

"Aura, what are you doing here?" he asked.

He was slightly startled when he realized that she was not wearing her scarf.

Oh, no! I must've left it at home!

Her mind was screaming, but she knew she couldn't lose control out in public. It would only drive more attention.

"Lord Blade," she said instead.

"Just Blade, please," he corrected her.

Aura crossed her arms. He was the last person she was expecting to see so soon.

"It's getting awfully late," said Blade. "You shouldn't be here alone."

The one who shouldn't be here alone is you, Aura thought. "I like to come here to think. I find the streets to be friendlier at this time. If people are sleeping, there is less noise, and so I feel that nothing else matters. "

Blade looked thoughtful. After a moment, he smiled. "I feel that way, too."

She looked at him with surprise.

"To be honest, I never really felt welcomed at Vesunna. I wasn't the child they wanted. I wasn't Blackwell's child, and I'm reminded of that every day. That's why I'm so intrigued by you. We're the same."

"The same?" Aura almost shouted. "How could you possibly say that we're the same? You're of royalty, handsome, and rich. I'm nothing but a poor peasant girl with a deformed face!"

He reached out a hand and touched her. From the expression on his face, she assumed that he was examining whatever deformity was on the skin of her cheek. She basked in the moment... but only for a few seconds. Then she turned her head away.

"Why are you being so nice to me?"

His face darkened. The smooth features turned into a wince.

"I learned about your story. And I know how you must feel. I still can't believe what happened. The queen is cold, for sure, but she also has a kind heart."

"Your queen is a monster. One even worse than me."

"You are not a monster," he said.

She cackled.

But he was serious. "My father says your mother went crazy. That she killed Lord Blackwell. And that because of that, she deserves to be killed as well."

Aura expected no less from the royal family. But coming from him, it felt worse. Like a betrayal. Like she was being stabbed in the heart. Even though she didn't know him, she felt terrible.

"He beat her, assaulted her. She had no other choice. My mother was forced to marry that man because this world makes life difficult for those who can't defend themselves."

Blade was silent at first. "Well, that's about to change."

"I don't see how."

"I'll show you," he said, nodding toward the plaza.

She looked at him suspiciously, then followed him down the alley and out into the square.

Once they were out in the square, Blade guided her through the market.

"What are we doing here?" she asked.

He said nothing and kept walking.

"Ignoring me won't make me leave you alone," she continued.

They continued walking until they finally turned the corner. There, they saw a labyrinth of the poorest people in Corconia, all lined up with what little they could sell for survival. These were difficult times. Even Aura, who was estranged from them, could understand the suffering of the villagers.

They passed a little seafood shop, with fish that didn't look fresh, then a produce shop, and finally, they found themselves in front of a family that was selling bread. Wherever they went, she saw people suffering.

Blade cleared his throat uncomfortably. "Here we are."

Finally, they stood in front of a shelter. Two children were seen walking hand-in-hand with an older girl, and further out on the playground, there were several children running and giggling.

"What is this place?" Aura asked.

"This is just something I do occasionally to help others. I don't like having a title. I want to earn the respect that comes with that title."

He looked so earnest. She wished she could believe him.

The older girl looked happy to see him.

"Blade!" she shouted and ran over to throw her arms around him.

Then she gave Aura a quick look. It was then that Aura saw how burnt her left cheek was. It was bad. The skin looked very burnt. A bright red X crossed her cheekbones and descended down her neck.

Blade's neck reddened.

"Aura, I want you to meet my sister. Her name is Indigo… and she is crushing me."

Indigo laughed and let go of her brother. Her soft curly hair fell like a curtain around her shoulders. She, unlike her brother, didn't look shy.

Indigo let go of Blade and extended her hand to greet Aura.

"Indigo Cross," she said, shaking Aura's hand.

"Aura," Aura responded.

"No last name? Interesting," she perplexed. "You're already a mystery. I like it!"

She was looking at her with recognition. Like she understood everything that Aura had gone through. Yet, she was standing in front of her with her pretty dress and a face that didn't seem to scare the life out of people who saw her. Hers was only an ugly scar on an otherwise beautiful face. There was simply no way they could compare.

She smiled at Aura.

"I'm not really his sister, by the way. Blade and I met when my father worked for him. But they don't work together anymore because my father is ill." She gave them both a sweet smile, always eager and always happy. "But enough about me. Did you come here to help us?"

Aura couldn't believe how normal it all seemed. This was the opposite of what she expected Blade to be like.

Then Indigo showed her where the other children were, and she entertained herself watching Blade wash dirty dishes in the little kitchen. His hands were filled with soap and water when Aura approached him.

"I didn't realize Lords were required to help others," Aura said.

"They are. Very much so. But it's also what I want to do. No one is forcing me."

"Is that why you come to Corconia so often? For this? For Indigo?"

Blade nodded. "Yeah, I didn't think bragging about how much I loved shopping was going to fool anyone, but it was all I could think of." Then he splashed some soapy water at her.

She giggled and splashed him back.

Soon, Indigo joined in, and the three of them engaged in a war of water and bubbles. It was the most fun she had in a long time. It made her feel like she belonged. It made her feel human.

And when she glanced at him and found him staring at her, she quickly turned her back to him.

"I have to go," she mumbled.

Being close to him felt wrong. So wrong, but so difficult to resist.

"Aura, wait!" He ran after her, stopping her right when she got to the door, and grabbed onto her arm.

"Hey, Aura, I'm sorry for what Queen Azra did to you, but I promise I'm going to show you that I'm not like that."

She pushed him aside, tears flowing down her cheeks when she stared him in the eyes.

"You don't want to follow me," she warned.

"I do! You still don't get that I'm not like the rest of my family, even after all this time?" he cried.

Aura hugged herself. Why couldn't he just understand that she was running away because she didn't want to hurt him?

"How can you say that? With a little bit more power, you'll become just like the rest of them. How do I know I can trust you?" Aura yelled back.

"Because I know how to break the curse," he said.

That made her pause.

"Really, you do?" she whispered.

He came closer to her. Now, they were only mere inches apart.

"Yes, I know all about it, and I know how to break it. I care about you, Aura, and I want to help you," he replied.

To her surprise, he leaned in even closer. Before she could say another word, she found his lips on top of hers, his mouth so gentle and so warm, unlike all the other men she had ever kissed. No, this wasn't just another kiss to kill. This was a kiss of love, of passion, and he did so without expecting the possibility of something more afterwards. He was kissing her for her, not for her eyes, not for her body, but for her.

Aura blushed. She had never felt such an emotion before. She didn't know what love felt like, but this was probably the closest thing to it. She found herself kissing him back, wrapping her arms around his neck and pulling him in closer. During that moment, all the thoughts of her curse and how much she despised the royal family vanished from her mind. All she could focus on was how maybe, just maybe, she could finally have a chance at love. She felt something tingle inside of her. It was like her heart was going to beat out of her chest, and she loved every second of it.

Then she pulled away. "You don't understand. I'm a monster. And it isn't only because of the way I look. I have done things I don't want anyone to know about."

But he didn't care. He continued to hold her in his arms, his fingers locked together around her waist.

"Me, too. I have stolen and lied to get power. So has everyone else before me. What you have done can't possibly be worse than that," Blade said.

"I have killed!" she screamed.

It was all just a little too much. She couldn't hurt someone like him. Not now. Not after hearing him say so many things that she wasn't expecting him to say. Not after their intimate moment.

"Why are you being so kind to me?" she asked when she realized he still didn't run away. "Don't you care that I'm not normal?"

He shook his head. "Listen, Aura, I know you. I've seen you. I've followed you. I know what you're capable of. And after all that, I'm still not scared. I'm still here." He grabbed her hands. "Doesn't that mean something?"

"You mean... you know that I'm a—"

"Vampire? Yes. I've known for a while now. You're not very good at hiding it. I suspected it at first, but after what I've heard from Florin, I knew it had to be true. Nothing else could've possibly left all those bodies lying around. I knew there had to be creatures living around the woods, or so my mother told me when I was a child."

"Your mother is right," Aura said. "And we are hungry. There's nothing but hatred following us around."

"Was. My mother *was* right. She died when I was just a child. Too young and too tragic."

"I'm sorry," Aura said.

"Don't be," Blade replied. "It was a while ago."

"Why didn't you tell anyone? Why didn't you report me if you knew?"

"Because I have a confession. I, too, wish to seek revenge against Castle Vesunna. My father kicked me out of the castle years ago, and I'm not welcomed back. Because he doesn't want me to inherit any of the riches that Lord Blackwell left behind for him. So, he casted me away to live like a peasant. I had to learn everything about the curse and your mother from Florin. He's the son of Nicolo, the man who used to be my father's right-hand man."

It all made sense now, why he wasn't like the rest of his family. He didn't live the same way as them. He didn't have the same values.

She gave him a surprised look, then asked him, "If you're no longer welcomed at the castle, how in the world are we supposed to get revenge? They won't let you in."

He winked. "You, Aura. You're the secret weapon. With your strength and power, all the guards will simply drop like flies. Even combined, they're no match for you." He reached out and hugged her. "I believe in you. Together, we can take down Castle Vesunna."

When he pulled away, there was now a less innocent quality to his smile. It made her feel nervous. That she wasn't the only one holding onto dark feelings.

THAT NIGHT, AURA CLIMBED UP THE STAIRS TO HER mother's room. She knew this was a risky venture, but it was now or never. Although part of her believed that she was strong enough to succeed, a smaller part of her was scared. She had never gone up against a whole army before. Three, yes. Maybe even five, but a whole army of Lucerian guards? That was more than she could even count. She knew she had to say farewell to her mother while she still could. If she didn't, and she ended up perishing in battle, she knew her mother would collapse from shock. Who would care for her? Who would make sure she drank?

When she finally reached the bedroom door, she gave it three knocks so her mother would know it was her. Her entire life, everything had come in threes. Three knocks to enter. Three screams for help. Three blinks to kill. If anything ever came in twos or fours, Marietta would know to immediately run and hide. So on edge, Marietta was. Such a sad way to live.

"Come in," a voice called out.

"Mother?" Aura asked as she walked in, closing the wooden door behind her. "How's Terrence's blood treating you?"

"Darling, honey, I'm going to need you to bring me some more human blood soon. These jars are starting to run empty. I don't know how much longer I can last."

Aura sat beside her. The color in her mother's face had returned, and through her eyes, Aura saw hope, not death. It almost seemed like a crime for her to say what she was about to say next.

"Mother, no."

"No?"

"No, because pretty soon, you're going to be able to get it yourself. No more hiding. No more fear. You'll finally get to be a vampire again."

Marietta just stared at her daughter, her eyes blinking in confusion. "What are you saying? You know I can't. The queen—"

"Queen Azra will die. Along with the rest of the royal

family. Tonight. And Blade Cross is helping me. He says we can band and take down the kingdom together."

Suddenly, the look of confusion turned into a look of rage. "Cross? Blade Cross? But he *is* part of the royal family. Why the hell would he help you destroy his own family?" She gestured the rest of her blood at Aura. "Drink this. I think you're growing delusional."

But Aura pushed back. "No, Mother. He *was* part of the royal family. Not anymore. They rejected him, built fury inside of him. He's like me. And he's going to help me."

"Okay, daughter, tell me this. Say he really isn't just a snake trying to trap you. How do you two expect to get through the army of guards at Castle Vesunna? They'll burn you, just like they burned your grandfather."

"Blade says I'm strong enough to take them down. He believes in me."

That's when Marietta cackled. "You? Take down the entire army? Aura, are you that foolish? Don't you see? He's manipulating you! He's just like his father. I was foolish and naïve enough to fall for it. I refuse to let you fall to the same fate." She spat on the ground. "That conniving snake!"

"He's not a snake! He's compassionate and kind. And I know he cares about me. Just because you were stupid enough to fall for someone else's tricks doesn't mean I'll do the same!" She knew that had hurt her. Time and time again, she had managed to disappoint her mother. But she had no other choice. It was either disobey her mother or be stuck in this curse forever. She simply had no other choice.

She walked out of the room, down the stairs, and headed out the door. Before closing it behind her, she turned back around and whispered, "Goodbye, Mother. If I don't see you again, please know that I love you."

Blade was standing outside her home when she walked out, suited in armor and perched on top of a mare. He looked like a knight, a knight who had come to save her, and all her worries about him washed away from her thoughts.

"My lady," he said, reaching out a hand to help her up.

He was so strong, so polite, that it warmed her heart. When she wrapped her arms around his torso, shivers tingled up her spine. She felt like she belonged on that horse with Blade.

Maybe I am capable of being loved.

The towns of Marsonia and Corconia were twenty miles apart, and cutting through the dense forest was the easiest way to get there. Aura pulled her hood further over her eyes when they passed a group of men. She assumed they were there looking for their dead friends, the ones she'd devoured. She couldn't bear to look at them, not because they'd recognize her or scream at her appearance, but because seeing her prey always made her hungrier. And she was hungry now! But she didn't want to kill in front of Blade, especially not innocent bystanders. She had to quell her thirst until they reached the castle.

An hour later, they arrived in Hibernia. Aura looked around. It looked exactly like how her mother had described it to her. The roads were battered up. Homes were torn down. And Aura had never seen so many people sleeping on streets, especially not on top of one another. She felt so awful. All her life, she thought her mother was trying to ruin her life, telling her what she could and could not do. She hated Marietta for it. But looking at the conditions in which she grew up, she couldn't help but admire her mother. She had gone through so much and still made it out alive. If Aura had lived here as a child, she wasn't sure she'd make it. There were corpses lying on the roads, for Heaven's sake!

"Blade," she turned to him and said. "Would you mind if we made a quick stop?

Blade looked at his watch. 11:28pm. They had planned on

arriving at Castle Vesunna by midnight, when Aura's ravenous senses were at their prime.

He nodded. "We can spare a few minutes."

She pointed him in the direction of the cabin where her mother used to live. Although her mother had never visited, she always told stories about all the wonderful times she'd spent there with her own mother, and how as much as she wanted to, she couldn't go back. It'll only bring back horrendous memories of Desdemona.

When they arrived, the lights were out. She knocked, but was answered by no one. She then knocked several more times, and the door soon creaked open. It was completely dark inside, and there was so much dust in the room that the two of them started to cough.

"Are you sure we should be in here? What if the owner comes back?" Blade asked.

But Aura only shook her head. She lit her torch and looked around. On top of the mantle, she saw several picture frames, many of her mother, her grandmother, and some strange woman.

"Why are these still here?" she whispered, dusting one of the frames with her finger. It was a picture of her mother as a child, standing next to a woman who looked like an older version of her. "Grandmother."

Setting her torch aside, she removed the photo from its frame, folded it, and shoved it in her pocket. She wanted her family with her, to be there for her and support her when she goes to Luceria.

"And what do you think you're doing?" a voice screamed, followed by the sound of the front door slamming open, a few nails popping off their hinges.

Blade nearly dropped his torch, and Aura jumped, the frame in her hands smashing onto the ground.

The scratchy voice belonged to an old woman, with her

shaggy gray hair draped over her shoulders and torn rags wrapped around her fragile body. But despite her appearance, the woman resembled the one who stood next to her grandmother in a few of the photos. Could it be that they all knew each other?

Then Aura shook her head. *No, it can't be. Even if she was, this woman was at least thirty years older than what she should be. She can't be her.*

"What are you? Mute?" the woman shouted again, walking up closer to Aura. "What are you two rascals doing in my house?"

"Um... sorry, ma'am. My mother used to live in this house. I just wanted to come by and see what it looked like."

That's when the woman's expression changed. "Your mother? No, no, no. I've lived in this house my whole life. No one else lived—" Then she paused, inched closer, and peered deep into Aura's eyes. "You're Desdemona's child? I thought she only had one evil spawn. Don't tell me there's another one!"

"Desdemona? No, but she's my grandmother. My mother is Marietta. Did you know them?"

The woman sighed. She slowly strolled over to the kitchen, lit a candle, and sat on one of the chairs. "Unfortunately, yes, and I've been haunted by their memories ever since. I'm Morgana."

"Morgana," Aura whispered. She didn't know much about Morgana. Her mother never wanted to speak of her, something to do with the horrid acts she had done. But she had heard the name before, followed by mutters of insults and words of hate. "No, it can't be. You can't be Morgana. You're much too old. It doesn't add up!"

"Hey! You don't see me judging your ugly face!"

Aura whispered her apologies and pulled her scarf further

up her face. Morgana could see her deformities, and all of a sudden, all her insecurities came rushing back.

"I *am* Morgana," she continued. "And I only look this way because of Queen Azra. I'm sure you know by now that your mother and grandmother are abnormals, and you're probably Marietta's cursed first born. You see, I was best friends with Desdemona, your grandmother, and they both lived with me for years. But I was living a secret, a lie."

She paused to take a sip of water, coughing a fit when the water traveled down the wrong way. "Unbeknownst to Desdemona, I was working for Queen Azra. She had captured my parents to work for her when the royal family invaded, and she threatened to kill them unless I helped her. She dug into my past. She knew! That evil witch. I didn't know why at first, but then when Desdemona told me what Marietta really was, I just froze. I didn't hate her for being the mother of an abnormal. I always thought she was a little... special. But with the guards standing there also, I had to let her go. I had to watch as they dragged my best friend off to die! Just like I had to watch helplessly when Queen Azra put the spell on your mother. I was powerless."

If Aura didn't feel so sorry for the pathetic old woman, she would've immediately pounced on her and ripped her entire face off. "That doesn't explain why you're so old."

"Queen Azra," Morgana said again. "Right after your mother was banished, I foolishly tried to kill the queen. She had taken away everyone I loved, even killed my parents right in front of me. I did her evil bidding, and all for nothing. But the queen is strong. She knew what I was up to right away. She put a spell on me, cursed me, turned me into this old and feeble woman, and then banished me to the forest forever where I can never leave. If I try, my body would instantly dissolve. Doesn't matter, anyway. It's not like I deserve to live. I've been living with this regret every day since."

Aura couldn't believe what she was hearing. All this time, she thought Morgana was this terrible person filled with nothing but hate and betrayal, but she had no other choice. To be honest, she would've probably done the same.

"Morgana, I need your help." She rested her hands on the woman's bony shoulders. "I need you to tell me Queen Azra's weakness. I need you to tell me how to destroy her."

Morgana swiftly pulled away, her eyes wide in horror. "No, my sweet child. You can't! If you even try and go near her, she will kill you. She's very powerful, more powerful that you think. Even your mother wasn't strong enough to withstand her powers!"

"I'm stronger than my mother, much stronger. And even if she does kill me, I'd rather try and die than live with this curse the rest of my life. Do you know how humiliating it is living with an appearance that people run from?!"

Morgana bowed her head. "I do now."

"Then you have to help me! Tell me what Azra's weakness is. How do I take her down?"

But the old woman remained silent, her head still bowed toward the ground.

"Fine, I don't need your help. I can deal with her myself." She opened the front door and turned back around. "You know, for someone who regrets what she did, you're not doing a whole lot to make up for it," she sneered and slammed it shut behind her.

When she walked back outside, she saw Blade kneeling on the icy grass. She was wondering where he'd gone.

"Blade?" she called out.

"Aura! Come here. Look what I found!"

When she reached him, he held out a necklace with a thin silver chain and small trinket in the center.

"It's beautiful," she said. "Is this yours?"

He shook his head. "It belongs to some woman named Desdemona. Do you have any idea who that is?"

Aura gulped. "Yes, she's my grandmother." She took the necklace from him and read the inscription on the back.

To my beautiful Desdemona
Love, Vladimir Covici

She didn't know she was crying until drops fell on the sleeves of her cloak. She couldn't believe it. It was a gift from her grandfather to her grandmother. It must've fallen off when the guards dragged Desdemona away. But the discovery didn't make her sad. Instead, it ignited a fire within her, a fire now desperate for revenge as she gripped tighter onto the necklace.

"I will avenge my family."

"CRISTIAN, MY GOOD MAN. WHAT DO YOU SAY WE GO grab a drink after our shift? Marius told me about this new saloon that just opened up. Tons of sexy ladies."

"Don't you have a wife and daughter, Mihai? What happens if Izabela finds out what you're up to?"

Mihai shook his head. "Nah, she won't. I've been able to get away with it for this long. She'll never find out. Besides, I don't believe in karma. So, what do you say? Drink?"

No answer.

"Cristian, why aren't you answering me?" Mihai turned around, ready to unleash his frustration on his partner, but instead, he saw Cristian lying on the ground and covered in blood. His neck was gashed open, his skin pale, and his body shriveled like a grape.

"Cristian? Cristian!" Mihai rushed over to the body. "Cristian, no, no, what happened?"

He tried picking up the body, but the coldness of it made

Mihai immediately drop it back down. He quickly stood up and backed into a tree, too in shock to decide whether he should run away or call for backup. He couldn't just leave his post. The queen would have his head if a Hibernian slipped through.

Lucky for him, he didn't have to make that decision. Before he could act, Aura leapt out from the other side of the tree he was leaning against and impaled him with her sharp white fangs, biting into his flesh until she felt bone. She was like a hungry animal. Once she got the taste of blood, she couldn't stop, not until everyone's gone.

She didn't even notice Blade watching with a grin on his face until after she finished Mihai and wiped off her mouth. He tasted sour, just like his personality.

"What's with the smile?" she asked.

Blade shrugged. "Nothing, just the way you attack. It's so riveting, almost like a work of art."

Aura raised a brow and glared at him. "Me killing people is a work of art?"

A siren blared before Blade had a chance to respond.

"Shit, they must've added extra security!" Aura grabbed Blade, bolted across to Luceria, and ran up a tree. They both sat there, perched like a nest, as they watched a dozen guards rush toward the breached wall.

"Search everywhere!" one of the guards ordered. "Shoot if you see movement. No hesitation."

"Yes, sir," the rest acknowledged and scattered throughout the premises.

"Why didn't you tell me that they installed alarms?" Aura nearly pushed Blade off the branch when she nudged him.

"They must've done it after I left. I swear, I didn't know!" He looked behind him. More and more guards were charging toward the wall. With their tree surrounded, the only place to go was up. "Aura," he said, gesturing to the roof of one of the nearby homes. "If you can make it over to that roof, I know a secret passageway to get inside the castle."

She looked over to where he was pointing. It was a long shot, with an eighty-five percent chance she won't make it, but she had to trust him. There was no other way out. So, she nodded.

"I can try. I might not make it, but I can try."

He smiled, brushing aside her hair. "I believe in you, Aura. You're stronger than you think." Then he leaned in to kiss her.

"Well, that certainly helps." She smiled back. "Hop on."

With Blade on her back, she aimed her vision to the spot she needed to land on. One mistake, and they'd be caught for sure. She closed her eyes and thought back to her mother, how much pain she suffered through, and how she was still able to remain strong. Opening her eyes again, she look a leap of faith, soaring through the air, before landing feet first on the other side.

I made it!

The secret passageway was nothing more than a tunnel underground, leading from the wall into the furnace room of Castle Vesunna. If Aura wasn't already so used to the darkness, she'd be scared out of her mind. But in a way, the absence of light was almost comforting to her, as if the lack of sight removed all the chaos from her mind. In the darkness, it felt like nothing was wrong.

"If my calculations are correct, then we should be right under the queen's corridor," Blade whispered.

He reached up and pushed against what seemed like a wooden door. "Ugh, it's stuck."

"Here, let me try," Aura offered.

Blade stepped aside, and she pressed her rough hands against the flat surface. With all her strength, she pushed, her arms buckling and her teeth gritting until the lock finally unlatched. They both climbed through and found themselves staring at none other than Lord Cross himself.

~

"I STILL MISS HER," CROSS WHISPERED TO HIMSELF while sitting on his gold-stained and jewel-embedded throne.

He sighed as he stared at a picture of himself and Marietta, the two of them smiling with his trusty stallion, Horseshoe, standing behind them. Horseshoe had died from old age over six years ago, leaving Cross devastated. He'd been with that stallion ever since he was a little boy. It had been the horse he trained on, the one his mother forced on him to learn. And even though he resented his mother for doing so at first, him and Horseshoe soon bonded, and they'd been inseparable ever since. The stallion had not only been his method of transportation but also his friend. But now, he was gone, much like any joyful memories he had left of Marietta Covici.

He remembered that day well, that day they took the picture. After the long journey to get as far away from Marsonia as possible, they finally arrived in Valeria, excited to celebrate their new life together.

If only that plan hadn't fallen through, things would be different now.

But he knew that was a lie. Even if Valeria hadn't turned out to be nothing but a dump, he still would've turned on Marietta. It would've taken some time, but she would've slipped up eventually. Sooner or later, she would've killed, just like her father, and he would've been forced to dispose of her in order to maintain his position on the throne.

And pregnant? He still couldn't believe it. What would the kingdom say if they found out he had bore an abnormal child? It would be his head on the guillotine. No, he couldn't risk that, and every day, he prayed that Marietta got rid of it.

She was cursed. It would be insane to bring that into the world.

But child or not, he never stopped thinking about the woman who stole his heart, the woman he fell in love with even before he found out that stealing her from his brother would result in him becoming the next king.

The year was 1949, and the vast array of fireworks shooting into the sky signified the start of the new year. Cross had grown tired of the parties and events in Luceria, with people who did nothing but stick their noses into other people's businesses, and decided to venture across the wall into Hibernia. He'd never been before; his time trapped in the east when his mother conquered Marsonia. He was nervous. Eager, but nervous, hearing nothing but horror stories from Blackwell about how the Hibernians ate each other for sustenance and killed because of hallucinations. But he wasn't scared. He'd always been adventurous, and he was excited to see what the western part of town had to offer.

Similar to the east, Hibernia also had parties of their own, just not as lavish. Instead of fireworks shooting into the sky, people threw confetti into the air. Instead of loud music and fancy attire, people wore their Sunday best and sang on the streets. It was a sight to see, and Cross soon felt out of place in his suit and overcoat.

Then he saw her. Out of the corner of his eye, he saw the most stunning girl walking toward him, the skirt of her dress gliding along the asphalt, and her beautiful long hair blowing against the wind. She was with a woman who looked like an older version of herself, and they were singing off-key. He smiled. Even with her lack of melody, she was still the most beautiful woman he had ever seen.

And when Blackwell decided to choose her, out of the thousands of eligible women in Marsonia, he was pissed.

Being the oldest, his brother had his first pick of the litter, selecting the one woman he wanted as his wife.

She was supposed to be mine, he thought, gripping tighter onto the photo. *He was supposed to choose a Lucerian, always flirting with them like he couldn't get enough, and I was supposed be with Marietta.*

Ever since, Lord Cross had resented his brother. He knew he had a crush on Marietta also, and he decided to choose her anyway. And to think he almost questioned his humanity when he felt no grief during his brother's funeral.

"Marietta," he whispered to himself. "I'm not even sure if you're still alive, but if you're still out there, I hope you can one day forgive me. I don't deserve you. I've done nothing but hurt you."

Suddenly, the floor began to rattle, and his room began to shake.

"Guards!" he shouted, backing himself into one of the walls to keep himself from tumbling over. "Nicolo!"

Nicolo, his loyal guard, rushed into the room with a small army of soldiers, all armed and ready to mutilate whoever was trying to break in. But when they entered, half the group fell over, the ground shaking so much that they struggled to keep their balance.

"What the hell's going on?" Cross shouted from across the room. He grabbed onto the pole of his bed and hung on for his dear life. He watched as the soldiers, one by one, flew across the room, and he didn't want to be next. "Make it stop! Make it stop!"

Then it stopped. The room stopped rattling, but it had been replaced by whispers. The whispers were soon followed by the floorboards creaking and slowly rising. Cross grabbed onto Nicolo, hiding behind him from whatever was about to rise from the ground.

"Father, don't shoot!" Blade yelled as the army pointed their guns at him. "It's me, Blade."

Cross nearly fell over. He couldn't believe who he was seeing, the son he thought had died, the son he thought he had lost forever.

"Blade? Is that really you?" He then rushed over to hug him, wrapping his arms around his son before Blade pushed him away.

"No, father, you didn't want me, and we didn't come here for a reunion. We came here for revenge."

"I... I didn't want you? What are you talking about, son? You ran away. Your grandmother told me that you ran away, and she even sent the guards out to find you. I thought you were dead!"

Blade crossed his arms over his chest, the stern look on his face unmoving. "Is that what she told you? From what I heard, you never wanted me, that you only had me because I was a prostitute's child, and that you never cared about me. She told me the guards took me away on your orders!"

"Son, please, you have to believe me. Your grandmother. She's evil. I never wanted any of this to happen." He tried hugging Blade again, but was interrupted by the sound of a female voice.

"Don't listen to him, Blade. He's lying. He's only manipulating you, just like he did to my mother," the young woman beside him said. She looked strangely familiar, like he had seen her before, a familiar face beneath all the scars.

"Your mother? I don't know your mother." He turned to Blade. "Son, believe me, please. Who are you really going to believe, your own father, or some girl who looks like she'd just been in battle?"

"My mother," she interrupted again. "Marietta. You ruined her life, lied to her, and destroyed her. And because of you, I now have to live with this wretched curse. You. You are going to die. Tonight!"

Cross couldn't move a muscle when he heard the words escape her mouth. *Marietta. So, this must be... no...*

"You're her, the child..." He was still in so much shock that he forced himself to sit down. His knees were buckling under his weight, and his heart was beating so fast that he felt like he was having a heart attack.

"Guards, seize her," Nicolo ordered.

"No! Stop!" Lord Cross intercepted, holding out his hand as the soldiers started to move.

"But sir." Nicolo walked over to his leader. "If we don't, she'll kill you."

Cross shook his head. "No, I don't care. I deserve it."

"Sir, why are you trying to protect this woman?"

And that's when he said the four words that stunned everyone standing in the room. "Because she's my daughter!"

And no one was more stunned than Aura herself. The intense rage temporarily left her body, replaced with confusion and so many questions.

"You're lying!" she yelled, but she couldn't tell for sure. Now that he was looking directly at him for the very first time, it was all beginning to make sense, why she didn't have a single resemblance to her father. She felt a lump begin to form in her throat.

"No, I'm not," Cross answered. "I *am* your father. And I was there when my mother cursed yours. I denied you. I denied the both of you, and I stood there, doing nothing, while Marietta was taken away. I refused to accept responsibility for you because I didn't want to lose the crown. Your mother was my first love, and instead of loving her back, I made the queen think she was a prostitute."

"Wait, father, is this true?" Blade stepped in and asked. "If she's your daughter, that... that means we're half-siblings??"

Cross nodded, "I'm afraid so."

Aura now felt the rock beginning to rise. *Half-brother?* She didn't know whether to kill them all for continuing to ruin her life or vomit at the fact that she had fallen in love with her own brother. But of course. If something like this were to happen to anyone, of course it would happen to her. She always had the worst of luck.

She looked over at Blade while he was still processing his life with his father, and she couldn't help but still feel butterflies in her stomach. Even though they were related, she still felt herself gravitating toward him. He had been the only man to ever love her, and although she knew why, part of her still wanted to be with him.

But love wasn't her goal. It never was. Love was just something she'd always longed for but never thought she'd achieve. No, revenge was her goal. This family had done nothing but destroy her family, killing them and sentencing them to die. She was so close. She had to avenge her mother.

And with one leap, she grabbed onto Nicolo, sinking her teeth into his pale neck before ripping out his veins. Nicolo screamed and fell to the ground, his body heaving heavily as he tried to fight back, but Aura was much too strong. But even with her strength, she was no match for the soldiers. They were all armed, from head to toe, and before she could even watch Nicolo die, she blacked out.

Nine

Marietta felt her heart break when she heard the front door slam, followed by the gallops of a horse. Carefully, she rose from her bed and looked out the window, watching her daughter ride away into the forest. The moon was shining bright, with the stars twinkling beside it. Her mother used to tell her that each star represented one of her ancestors, all just as magical as she was, and how one day, she'd join them up in the skies. As a kid, she'd laughed at the stories; now, looking up at her mother and father in Heaven, she longed to join them.

But she couldn't leave her daughter behind, nor could she bear to watch Aura ascend without her.

She sighed and lied down in bed. *With her craziness, she'd get herself killed one of these days.*

But something was bothering her. She couldn't rest. Not with Aura out for blood at Castle Vesunna. Marietta knew the horrors that went on inside there, and just how powerful the guards were. There's no way she could take them all on, not even as a vampire.

But she's tenacious, strong-willed. Maybe I'm just worrying too much. I'm sure she'll be fine.

"No!" She threw the covers off her head and changed out of her nightgown. "I have to save her... even if it kills me."

Marietta hadn't gone back to Marsonia ever since that day, especially not back to Castle Vesunna. She was banished, excommunicated. And if anyone ever caught her there, she'd be burned at the stake. No one could save her, not even Cross. Especially not Cross.

Her anxiety burned through her stomach as she raced across the dark forest. With nothing but her two feet to travel on, it took her days to reach the castle, stopping every several miles to replenish her essence. As she drank, she didn't know why she'd been so scared. The worst Queen Azra could do was kill her, and if she didn't feed, she was good as dead anyway. The blood tasted like sweet nectar as it traveled down her throat, and she felt more powerful and vibrant than ever.

DAYS LATER, SHE FINALLY ARRIVED. JUDGING BY THE number of soldiers who stood guarding the wall, she knew Aura must've breached it. And if she was already inside the castle, she may already be dead. Marietta looked around, from one side of the wall to the other, trying to find a gap she could sneak through, or at least, an area with less security. Nothing.

Don't worry, honey. Mother's coming.

She knew she couldn't just walk up to the wall and start killing. There were too many of them, and she'd never be able to make it out alive. The only other option was diversion, make them think that someone else was intruding so she could sneak by.

The man in the woods.

She traced back her steps. *I know I left him here... somewhere.*

Marietta continued walking until she tripped over a stump and fell, scraping her knee and bruising her spirit. Just when she was about to curse the tree, she realized that it wasn't actually a tree. It was him!

She scooped up the body, draped it over her shoulder, and headed back to the wall. Ducking behind a thick tree, she heaved with all her might, and the body soared through the air and into the bushes on the other side.

"What was that?" She heard one of the guards say.

"Make sure no one breaks in! One more breach, and it's off with our heads," another one called out, and Marietta watched in pride as half the army rushed over to where the body landed.

But there were still a few left, a few fools left to guard the wall. It'd be a close call, but she was sure she could drain them without anyone noticing. She waited until the coast was clear, then snuck behind one of the men, pulled him aside, and drank from him. It was dark, so it made it more difficult to notice when someone was missing, which was only a bonus for her.

Four guards later, she was down to the last one. She looked over at the bushes, where the other guards were still searching, to make sure they weren't heading back. Marietta then bit down into the last remaining guard and threw him aside once he fell limp. Her hunger was strong, but not enough for the whole army.

But right when she thought she had made it, an alarm sounded when she grabbed one of the men's key and unlocked the gate.

Shit! That wasn't here last time!

She tried to run. She tried to scurry up a tree, hide behind the leaves, but it was too late. As soon as the alarm sounded, she was surrounded. The soldiers, all dressed in black with their faces covered by a mask, pinned her onto the ground and arrested her.

"Let me go! Let me go, you imbeciles! I need to find my daughter!" Marietta screamed as they dragged her into the dungeon of the castle. Her voice echoed throughout the halls, and the silence of the soldiers only added to the suspense. But it didn't matter. She could scream all she wanted. They didn't care about her or her daughter.

When they finally reached an empty cell, the noise from the clomps of their boots and jingles from their keys made it hard for her to hear herself. She tried to reason with them, plead for them to let her go, but they continued to remain silent and threw her inside the empty room.

"Are you going to kill me?" She asked, her fingers wrapped around the thin metal bars of the gate.

"The Lord will decide your fate," one of the masked men said. Then he turned around and walked away while other guards came over to watch her, to make sure she didn't escape.

The next morning, Marietta found herself still in the cell, lying in her own filth. She thought it was a dream, a nightmare, hoping she'd wake up wrapped in the comfort of her own sheets. Instead, she found herself wrapped in the stains of her victims' blood.

"Can I at least get some water? I'm parched," she called out to one of the guards, but he ignored her. "You know, for high-class snobs, you really should learn some manners."

She walked to the back corner of the tiny room and sat herself down, staring up at the rusty metal ceiling. The last time she was here, she experienced nothing but horrific experiences. This wasn't much better. And she definitely wasn't in the mood to see Queen Azra. She wondered how long her death would take, how long Azra would torture her before watching the skin melt off Marietta's face. She'd probably laugh, ridicule her for being so foolish and returning to Vesunna. Hell, she could be burning Aura right this moment. She didn't know. But at least if she died, she'd know she at least died trying. And that was enough to rectify her guilt.

Her thoughts were interrupted when a bell sounded. The chimes were so loud that it nearly deafened Marietta.

"All hail the Lord," the crowd of guards chanted as they saluted a shadow walking in her direction. She couldn't make out much, just a crown and a staff.

I see she hasn't humbled herself.

"What's the point?" she whispered to herself. "Why bother saluting her if she's going to kill me?" She stepped away from the bars and sat back in her corner, tearing into her skin with her nails to watch her own blood seep out.

"Marietta?" She heard a familiar voice ask. "Is that really you?"

She looked up, and there he was, the traitor himself. Cross.

"They said they caught an abnormal. I wasn't expecting it to be you when I came down here, but honestly, I'm glad it is."

Marietta looked at him, still as handsome as the day she first saw him, but her hatred for him was enough to overpower any lingering feelings she still felt toward the man. "Do you have my daughter?"

"Aura's safe, Marietta, I can assure you of that. She killed Nicolo, and she'll have to pay the consequences, but for now, she's safe."

She lunged to the bars, trying to grab Cross by the neck so she could strangle him. But his guards stood in the way, shielding and protecting him. "Give her back, you monster! You destroyed my life. Don't you DARE destroy hers, too! I should've never trusted you. Nicolo deserves to DIE for what he did. I wish you were dead, too!" She gave the bars a good shake, the sound rattling down the halls, and went back to the corner. "If you're going to kill me, then just kill me now. Otherwise, get the hell out of my face."

Cross didn't say another word. He bowed his head in respect and signaled for the guards to leave.

That night, the moon was out again, but the dungeon remained dark, not even a candle or flame to shed some light onto her miserable life. And Cross. She'd spent the past twenty-five years hating him, despising every bone in his body, wishing for the day when she could finally avenge the death of her mother and everything else he had done to her. Ever since that day, she swore to herself that the next time she saw him, she'd have his blood.

So, what's wrong now? Why didn't she feel any of that? Instead of hate, she found herself reminiscing of the times they were together, from how he threw rocks at her window and professed his love to her to how sensual he felt when they made love. As much as she wanted to kill him, she also still loved him, and she secretly wished that he hadn't turned out to be the snake that he was.

He had promised her the world, a journey to explore life outside Marsonia, just the two of them. But that had all been a lie. He used her, manipulated her, and then tossed her in the pits of Hell to care for their child. Cross was her first love, the man she thought would finally replace the absence of her father and save her from a life of slavery and punishment. She thought he was different from Blackwell, that he actually wanted more than just power. She couldn't have been more wrong.

"I miss him," she whispered to herself. "I wish I'd never met him because now, I can't stop thinking about him."

Then she spun around, "Who's... Who's there?"

A sliver of light shone in, blinding her for a second before she heard the creak of the door as it opened the rest of the way. The dungeon was much brighter now, with one side filled with light while the other side remained mysterious.

"It's me," the voice answered. "It's me, Cross."

Marietta felt her heart skip a beat. Could this be just a coincidence? Or had her thoughts of him summoned the man himself?

"I have nothing to say to you."

She wanted to say more, much more. She wanted to run toward him and tell him how she never stopped thinking about him, how she missed their times together. She also wanted to throw him a dagger of a thousand words and rip his heart out for the way he treated her. Instead, the constant struggle between her heart and her mind made her nothing more than indifferent.

"Marietta, please, let me explain. Just give me a few minutes of your time, and if you still despise me and want me to leave, I will, and I'll never bother you again."

She huffed. "Fine."

"Marietta, I know I messed up. I know you probably think I was only with you to use you. And I'll be honest, part of me was."

"I knew it! I fucking knew it!" she interrupted.

"I know, I know. But falling in love with you was never

part of the plan. I've loved you even before I knew I had a shot at the crown, but when all that started to come alive, when I knew I could be next in line, I just knew I had to take it." He bowed his head. "Even if it meant losing you."

"You denied me, Cross. You denied me and my child. You don't know what it's like, being alone, with child, and banished to where civilization had long died. And the worst part is, never did you try and find us, only caring about your stupid crown. For the past twenty-five years, I've struggled, with a daughter who resents me and living with the fear that if I tried to eat and survive, I'd be killed. God, Cross, I even killed your brother so I could be with you. Everything I did, for you. You didn't even come to find me. You married someone else instead, and had a kid with her! What, are you going to abandon him, too? Just like you did with Aura?"

"I thought you were dead," Cross replied as tears welled in his eyes. "I never tried to find you because I thought all hope was lost. I never thought I'd see you again."

She scoffed. "You didn't try; that's the problem. So, if you've come here to brag about how you stole your brother's crown and made me do your dirty bidding for you, save it. I'd rather end my own life than give you that satisfaction."

He shook his head. "No, I didn't come for that. After you left, things have never been the same. Sure, I got the power, the throne, the crown, but I didn't have everything. I didn't have you. I never stopped thinking about you, Marietta, and how I promised you the world then took it all away. I thought I wanted the power, a chance to rule the kingdom, but seeing you, after so long, I'd rather give it all up than risk losing you again."

Marietta cackled. "Ha! You really expect me to fall for that? The last time I trusted you, I ended up paying for it with the life of my child. Fool me once. Never again."

"How can I make this right, Marietta? What will it take for you to forgive me?"

She looked over at his face. The dim light of the candle gave way to part of his expression. His face had fallen, and the devious look he had in his eyes when he betrayed her was gone. Sure, he seemed genuine, his apology almost sincere, but could she trust him? She missed him dearly, and a huge part of her wanted to spend her life with him, to be with him again and find love in each other's arms. He was telling her exactly what she'd always wanted to hear, an apology to take away all her hatred for him.

But what if he was lying? What if he was manipulating her again, playing with her heart for his own gain? What if she decides to trust him, and he turns her in to Azra instead?

She sighed. *Do I really have anything left to lose? I can either believe that there's still a sprinkle of decency left in him and that he's telling the truth, or I can sit here and waste away.*

Her stomach growled. It had been growling since last night, and she found herself desperate for her next feed. She thought of maybe just getting him to come close enough, so she could feed from him, but that wouldn't aid her in saving Aura. It would just make her a greater target for the queen.

"Our daughter," she finally said. "Help me save our daughter."

AURA WAS AWOKEN BY THE SOUND OF HISSING IN her ears and scales slithering along her skin. She peered open one eye and found herself in a pit, completely surrounded by squamates. Alert and frightened, she leapt up and tried to climb up the side, eventually grabbing hold of a loose brick to keep herself from being eaten alive. She looked down. There were at least five hundred of them, with several dozen making their way up the side.

"No!" she cried. "It can't end like this. Blade? Blade!"

But she was met with no answer.

"He betrayed me, didn't he?! Lured me into this castle with a sob story, just to watch me get eaten by snakes. I should've known. I should've listened to my mother. He's nothing but another Cross. They're all the fucking same."

Vomit rose up her throat as she remembered what Lord Cross had said. "Half-brother? And to think I actually kissed him?"

The sound of hissing suddenly turned to cheers and laughter. It echoed from where she was, and she heard the sound of beating drums marching to a rhythm.

"Welcome Lucerians! To the annual Kismet Chase!" The announcer's voice was hoarse, like he had either swallowed a toad or smoked an entire pack of cigarettes.

Kismet. She'd heard of it before, from her mother. It was where her grandfather had died, tackled, and destroyed like a ragdoll when he tried to fight for his people. But it wasn't something Aura, nor her mother, had ever experienced themselves. Men were always the chosen ones, a fair fight to see who the strongest of the weak were.

"And this year," the announcer continued. "We have a special surprise for all of you, a treat you've all been waiting for, an abnormal!"

"What?"

Before she could even register what was about to happen or why she was there, the pit began to rise, the darkness turning into light, and when she opened her eyes again, she saw the crowd. They were merciless animals, all rooting for her to die and throwing whatever they could find straight at her. She cowered, trying to dodge the sharp objects, but with her entire body locked in chains, there wasn't much she could do.

The guards wheeled her to the center of the yard, the epicenter of the event, where she saw Blade, suited in armor and strapped to a pole.

"Blade! What the hell is going on?" Aura shouted at him, realizing that he was in the same position as her, confined and helpless.

"I'm sorry, Aura, I tried to stop them. I tried to save you, but they got to the queen long before I could. I followed them, tried to stop them, but they soon knocked me out. I didn't regain consciousness until I woke up here. I'm so sorry, Aura, I really did try."

"I know," she whispered.

The announcer continued. "On the left side of the stadium, we have the abnormal, one powerful enough to take down half an army. On the right side, we have none other than a former member of the royal family, who has betrayed his people to the point of no return, and he shall now perish. Winner takes all and walks out of here alive. No mercy. Let the battle begin!"

As the soldiers unchained her, Aura contemplated all the possible ways she could sink her teeth into them, followed by the announcer spewing nothing but blasphemy. But then she thought back to her grandfather, who thought he could do the same but ended up paying for it with his life. She looked over at Blade, who was also untied, and now, with a sword in his hand.

"I don't want to hurt you, Aura." His voice was trembling, and his body was shaking.

Aura had a clear view of his neck, a small section where skin was exposed. She could easily rip him apart and walk out of this alive. That is, if Queen Azra was even planning on letting her live.

"Kill the freak!" She heard the crowd cheer.

She knew they were all rooting for Blade. And the smell

from his weapon made her suspect that something had spiked it so it would poison her.

Blade was an easy target, for sure. And normally, she'd have no problem ripping him into pieces, especially as her stomach rumbled for sustenance.

But something was holding her back. Her love for him. Even though they had the same father, she couldn't help but still care for him. She thought back to how he saw her and stayed when no one else ever had, how he loved her for her and not for what she could offer. After all that, how could she possibly end his life for her own selfish gain?

THE MAN GUARDING THE DUNGEON HALL WAS asleep. It took Marietta no time to snap his neck and leave him on the ground as she and Cross snuck out.

The queen was next.

"The guards brought Aura to her." Cross had said. "I don't know what she's planning on doing, but whatever it is, it won't be quick and easy."

They soon arrived at her corridor, the door slightly ajar. Marietta looked in to try and spot the queen, but she saw no one.

"How exactly are we supposed to break this curse?" she turned around and whispered.

Cross was standing close behind her, the air from his breath landing on her every second.

"The necklace," he replied. "The necklace around her neck. She never takes it off. It's the key to all her power. Without it, she's just another human being."

Marietta rolled her eyes in disbelief. "Are you serious? That sounds like a fantasy story."

"And vampires don't?"

"Okay, fine, you have a point. But how is finding the necklace supposed to end this?"

"Break the necklace, break the curse. Aura will no longer have a deformity, and the queen will become helpless, an easy kill." He pulled a dagger from his back pocket and pushed the door slightly further. It barely made a noise, and he gestured her to follow him.

"Cross, wait," Marietta said instead and held him back. "Why are you helping me? She *is* your mother, after all."

He smiled at her and brushed the side of her face with his empty hand. "True, she is my mother, but she's not family. In fact, she's been trying to destroy my family ever since I could remember. And when she got rid of Blade, that was the last straw. Besides, Marietta, I love you, and like I said, I'm willing to give up everything I have for you. And even if you decide to kill me after this, I'd at least die happy, knowing that I died at your hands and not someone else's."

Marietta shifted her weight closer to him. His words reminded her of the Cross she fell in love with, the one who stole her heart. She then leaned up and kissed him on the lips, gracing her lips against his and entangling their tongues together. He kissed her back, his hands on the small of her back as he pulled closer.

"Hmm, I don't know what that was for, but I'm not complaining," Cross said, and then leaned in for another.

She stopped him, putting her blade in between them, and grinned. "Not until we find her," she teased.

But when they pushed their way into the queen's room, it was empty. She wasn't there! Not even the guards who usually lined around corridor were there.

"Where is she?" Marietta hissed at the man standing beside her, who was equally confused.

Just then, they heard a rumbling sound coming from

nearby. The noise sounded foreign, but Cross seemed to recognize it. "Kismet!" he shouted.

Hearing that word gave Marietta a horrific sense of déjà vu. She could still remember the day her father died. He promised he'd come back, come back with more food than they could ever need, but he never came back at all. Marietta hated how naïve and imprudent she was, how she pushed her father to go because she wanted more than bread scraps for dinner. Now, she'd willingly nosh on stale bread the rest of her life if it meant she could have him back.

The long walk down the hall and out to the yard was treacherous. It reminded Marietta of her first visit to Castle Vesunna, when she thought she had to marry Lord Blackwell. Her life had changed so much since. Sometimes, she wondered how different everything would've been if she ended up wedding him, whether she'd even still be alive.

She knew they were getting close when the roars grew louder. Cross led her down to a spot below the bleachers so no one would notice them. Marietta almost screamed when she saw Aura standing in the middle of the field while Blade gripped tight onto a sword. Neither of them were doing anything. They both just stood there.

"We have to save them!" Marietta hissed again to Cross.

But he wasn't paying attention. His focus was on Queen Azra, who sat on her high throne, center stage, sipping on a glass of red wine, and smirking at the scene before her. Around her neck, Marietta noticed the necklace, the same cheap trinket that was dangled in front of her twenty-five years ago. If only she had known. If only she had known what that necklace actually meant, she wouldn't be here now.

"Ivan," Queen Azra called over one of her trusty guards. "Ivan, tell me, why aren't they fighting?"

"I'm... I'm not sure, your highness. They seem to be having a conversation. Maybe we need to do something to stir the pot."

"Yes," she acknowledged. "Whatever it takes. Our guests are growing tired and uninterested. This is our big event. If this fails, no one would ever return to Kismet."

"I'll get right on it, your highness. I believe the lions haven't been fed yet."

Azra poured herself another glass as Ivan walked away. She stared out onto the field, feeling no remorse as she pitted her two grandchildren against each other.

She'd always wanted grandchildren, from her eldest son, Blackwell, anyway. But ever since he died, her heart no longer welcomed them. She eventually found out that Marietta's child was Cross' daughter, a shame she continued to face ever since the realization. Her own blood giving life to an abnormal child. It was more than she could handle. His affair with the vampire had tainted his sperm, and he could never have a normal child. That's why she tried to get rid of Blade, a tarnished spawn of Marietta's remnants. But clearly, given the full-grown man standing before her, she hadn't done enough.

"Where did I go wrong? I fought through teeth and nail to give my sons a life they deserved, and this is how they repay me? With death and betrayal? I should've given them up when I had the chance."

Soon enough, Azra heard the sound of roaring wildcats, followed by the chains of barred gates opening. Three full lionesses waltzed out, following the buckets of steak the guards held in front of them, leading them toward Blade and Aura. They roared again, the sound of a thousand beasts strong in their tones, and Azra smiled to herself while gripping onto her glass, ready for the suspense. That spell she had put on those cubs really did their magic. She was worried it wouldn't work at first, but when they grew to be ten times their size in a mere three weeks, she couldn't help but pat herself on the back. She couldn't be prouder.

And so was the crowd. As one of the lionesses mauled through a piece of meat, she glared an eye at Aura. Probably the sweet, sweet blood of the abnormal. Those were usually difficult to resist. She continued watching as Aura backed away, with her fists clenched and ready to pounce on the beast. She tried leaping onto one, grabbing her by the neck, and cinching into it with her fangs, but it was no use. The lioness remained unscathed, charging again at her as she tried to take on lioness number two.

Azra laughed. "Silly, silly, child. Your powers are no match for mine. These beasts are indestructible... unlike you. One scratch from their deadly claws, and you're as good as dead."

"Don't move another inch," a voice said from behind her. "Unless you're prepared to die."

Queen Azra sat on her throne with all its glory, as insidious as the day they first met. Cross had told Marietta to remain discreet, the only way they'd be able to sneak the necklace off her without her noticing. Marietta tried to fight it, gritting her teeth and holding back her pent-up rage. She wanted nothing more than to tear into Azra's face with her sharp fangs and rip away everything that was important to her. Sure, she had forgiven Cross, but Queen Azra had a black heart. There was no chance in hell she'd ever feel remorse.

The blue necklace was hanging off her neck and catching the sun's rays. Even in its most beautiful state, it still looked like a cheap toy. She still found it hard to believe that all her power rested in that tiny plastic gem, but that was the only lead she had. She had to try for Aura; she owed her at least that much.

The queen was dressed in garments of blue and gold, with a large silver crown atop her head. Below her, guards surrounded her left and right, so the only way to get to her was from behind. When they got close enough, Marietta lifted her fingers. This was the first time her light and nimble fingers came in handy, gently tugging on the chain until the entire thing slid off.

"Don't move another inch," she said from behind the queen. "Unless you're prepared to die."

Queen Azra spun around, failing to notice the necklace missing from around her neck. "You!" she shrieked. "I thought I got rid of you decades ago! Guards, seize her!"

But Cross held out a hand to stop them as Marietta sneered. "I don't think so," she said, her eyes pointing to the dagger she held against her heart.

Getting this close to her was terrifying for Marietta. If Cross had lied to her, and Azra was still a witch even without her necklace, she would've accomplished nothing.

Azra screeched. "A dagger? You're even more foolish than you were over twenty years ago. Are you forgetting that I'm a Raven? Your little knife is no match for me. And you!" She pointed at Cross. "How dare you betray your own mother like this? I birthed you. I gave you everything, and you choose this harlot over me? Blackwell shouldn't have been the one to die. You should've."

The queen raised her hands and recited a few chants, cackling as she did so. "You'll both be sorry you ever came here." But when she lowered them back down again, nothing happened. "What?" She tried once more, but the same thing happened. Nothing. She then felt around her neck and dug her hands into her pockets as if she was looking for something. "Where is it? Where is it?!"

"Looking for this?" Marietta taunted, holding the necklace up in the air as Azra's eyes widened in horror.

Azra tried to grab for it, but before she could even get close, Marietta threw it against the ground and shattered the stone, a ray of blue soaring into the sky, turning lighter and lighter, until it disappeared. She looked over toward the center of the stadium and saw the lions turn back into cubs, pure creatures of the stone. She then swiftly grabbed the queen and ripped into her neck, blood pouring down her body and staining her clothes a scarlet red. Azra managed to pull away after that one bite, running away from the bleachers before Marietta could sink her teeth into her again.

"She's getting away!" Cross yelled, pointing at where his mother was pushing through the crowd.

"Let her go," Marietta answered calmly. "With that much blood loss, she won't make it very far."

As for the guards, it turned out that they were under Azra's spell this entire time, innocent citizens of Romania she had cursed into doing her bidding. And once the spell broke, they all looked equally confused, staring at each other and unsure of how they got there.

The audience of Lucerians, on the other hand, didn't remain as calm or confused. This generation had never witnessed an attack of a vampire before, and when they did, began screaming and pushing each other over to escape being next. Marietta chuckled to herself as she watched them flail across the field like wingless birds. *If only this world was a little more accepting of the abnormals.*

"Aura!" She suddenly remembered the reason she was even here. She rushed down the steps to find Blade's arms wrapped around her daughter.

"Aura, I mean, my daughter, my beautiful daughter. Your

face, the deformity, it's gone!" Cross exclaimed from behind Marietta.

Aura felt around her face. Although she'd never know what was different about her, something just felt... better. Like she was finally free of what was holding her back. She reached over and gave Marietta a hug.

"Thank you, Mother. You broke the curse."

Marietta hugged her back. "No, Aura. *You* broke the curse. If it wasn't for what you've taught me all these years, I would've never found the courage to do so."

Ten

They say a year isn't much, that not a lot can really change during that time, but for the town of Marsonia, that couldn't be less true. With Queen Azra gone and Lord Cross stepping down from the throne, the wall was torn down, and the Lucerians and Hibernians intermingled as neighbors and friends. No longer was Marsonia segregated between the east and the west, the rich and the poor. Merchants coming from sea were able to travel to the western part of town, and roads from the north were no longer blocked. The wealth of the upper class was shared with the lower class, and together, both sides rebuilt the community into what it used to be.

As for Castle Vesunna, it had been abandoned, now left as a tourist attraction for those who wanted a good story about all the horrors that happened behind those walls. The guards had returned back to their hometowns, and Lord Cross moved into a cabin by the Black Sea, with his wife, Marietta, and their two children.

He'd asked Marietta to marry him a month after the curse was broken, proving to her how much he'd changed and how he wanted to choose love over power. Blade and Aura remained friends. Their attraction for each other slowly faded as the realization that they were siblings became more and more real for them. But even so, they never forgot their first kiss.

But life wasn't completely normal for them. Marietta and Aura still ventured out at night as vigilantes, feeding on criminals and invaders. Many of the Lucerians never accepted their new way of life, so crime soared in Marsonia from what it used to be. But Cross and Blade never minded. They loved their counterparts regardless, and they wouldn't have it any other way. Life was beginning to look up for everyone, but like all good things, it wouldn't last long.

"Mother," Aura said during a dark and snowy night. The waves from the sea were beating against the shore, and trees swayed back and forth in unison. The Christmas season had always been their favorite time of the year, where darkness seemed to coat the Earth. "Father's been out for an awfully long time. Do you think he got lost?"

Marietta giggled. "You father never was good with directions. I'm sure he's just running a little late. Maybe the forest isn't so kind tonight, and he's having trouble collecting enough kindling."

"Perhaps I should go check on him," Blade offered. He

grabbed his coat from the rack by the door and turned the knob.

"Wait! I'm coming, too," Aura volunteered. "It's not safe out there. You need someone who's not afraid to kill when the night calls for it."

Blade rolled his eyes at her. "Just because I'm not an abnormal, doesn't mean I don't know how to protect myself."

Aura smiled. It always made her smile whenever he pouted. Even though she couldn't be with him romantically, he always had a special place in her heart.

"Aura, what's it like being a vampire?" Blade asked as they walked into the forest in search of their father. "I mean, does it hurt?"

She threw him a look. "Does it hurt? What? Does it hurt being a human? What the hell kind of question is that?"

"Sorry." He shook the dusting of snow off his head. "I guess I meant to ask, can you bite me? So, I can become like you?"

She raised a brow. "You want me to turn you into a vampire? Why?"

"Death," he answered. "It's always scared me. And with all the murders in Marsonia lately, I may not have much time left. And I can't have you hanging around me all the time, protecting me. It's embarrassing!"

"Blade... I don't know. I can't. I can't do that to you."

"Aura, please! Don't you care if I die? I've never asked you for anything except for this. I've been there for you. I've loved you, and all I ask for in return is one single bite. Can't you at least give me that? I can't believe you'd be so selfish."

He was right. He'd been there for her when no one else had, not even her own mother. But part of her still loved him, not just as a brother, and she feared that if she turned him, all his innocence would be lost, and he wouldn't be the same Blade she once knew.

"Blade," she whispered. "I need to tell you something." She reached out and grabbed his hand to keep him from moving forward. "I'm not trying to be selfish. And I know this may scare you away, but the real reason why I can't turn you is... is... is because I still have feelings for you. I know it's wrong, being that you're my brother and all, but before I knew that, I thought I'd found my soulmate, in you. And I can't find it in myself to bite you because I'm afraid that will change you, and I don't want you to change. I love you for you."

Her face blushed, and she turned around. She took a deep breath as Blade stepped up behind her and wrapped his strong arms around her. "I know how you feel," he whispered in her ear.

"You do?"

He nodded. "It's such a shame that we have the same father, but I don't think that should stop us from caring about each other. Aura, I've loved you since that first day at the market. Even with your deformity, I fell for you, and I haven't stopped since. And I don't think we should let the fact that we're blood ruin what we had." He leaned down and kissed the side of her face. "I love you, Aura, and I promise you that I'll never change, even if I turn. Because I'll always have you here to keep me grounded, to remind me of who I am."

She turned around and looked up at him. Even as a human, his smile was alluring, blinding, and enchanting. If he turned, his senses would become that much more enhanced.

Maybe it wouldn't be so bad after all, she thought.

"Are you sure?" she asked. "What if you regret it after it happens? It would be impossible to turn you back, and I don't want you to resent me. Being a vampire doesn't come with the glitz and glam of what you hear about in stories. It's a life of constant bloodlust and anger, of vice and loneliness."

"I know, but it's also a life of safety and protection, and I need that. You, of all people, should know how important it is to be able to defend yourself without having to rely on someone else." He pulled her closer into a hug. "I'm scared, Aura. I'm scared of death, and if you turn me, I'd at least know I have better means of protecting myself." He pulled down one side of his collar. "Please, Aura, please do this for me."

She hesitated. She didn't want to hurt him, but she also knew he was right. Besides, he looked so happy and so confident in his decision. She couldn't disappoint him, not after what he had done for her.

"Are you sure?" she asked.

He smiled deeply.

"Of course, I'm sure," Blade said.

And it was then, when she decided to sink her teeth into him. She touched his neck softly.

"I don't know if it'll hurt," she said.

"Pain's necessary for all things good," he assured her, then touched her face when she came closer to his neck. "And I'm willing to risk pain for this. For you."

She swallowed. He smelled delicious. Like old spice and cedarwood, but with a stronger note. Touching his neck with her lips, she planted soft and gentle kisses on him. She wanted to savor the way his body tasted before anything happened, be with him one last time as a human. Their bodies merged closer together, Blade trying to hold himself back from doing anything he'd regret, and Aura whispering "I love you" into his ear one last time before sinking her teeth into his skin. He winced, and his body slightly jerked, but he didn't pull away. He succumbed to the sharpness of her fangs, letting his body fall victim to her. He grabbed onto her body as she sunk her teeth deeper, the pain growing as she did, their arms embracing each other as they became one.

When she finally pulled away, blood seeped from neck. Aura leaned back over, sensually drinking the remnants of it before asking him how he felt.

"I don't feel any different... a little tingly and lightheaded, but I don't feel stronger or more alert. I don't feel like a vampire."

"Don't worry. Most of the time, I don't either, only when I'm hungry. It's not like we have these special senses that we feel all the time. Other than the desire for human blood, we're just like the humans."

He pulled her toward him again and kissed her other cheek. "Thank you, Aura. Now, what do you say we go rescue the old man?"

Less than fifty feet later, Aura scrunched her nose. "Hey, Blade, do you smell that?"

He sniffed. "You mean the wintergreen?"

"No, something smells... rotten? I think it's coming from over there."

She pointed toward the rock Cross always loved sitting on whenever he needed a break from gathering lumber. He always joked around and called it his new throne. Aura and Blade didn't understand the humor of it, but it usually gave Marietta a good chuckle.

As they approached closer to the rock, they noticed an unusual swarm of flies in the area. It was odd, especially during the winter season. But when they followed the flies around back, they saw a sight that made Blade hurl. It was Lord Cross, or at least, what was left of him. His head had been decapitated, and his body had been torn into shreds.

Aura screamed, and Blade dropped his knees to the ground to mourn his father. He pressed his hands against the remains of Cross' arm, praying that this was all just a nightmare.

"Father, no, it can't be. Please wake up. Please wake up!"

He cried out while Aura looked around, trying to spot the beast that did this.

"I don't understand," Aura said. "Who could've done this? And why?"

She continued to pace, determined to track down the animal that did this and end its life for good, when she noticed a snag of fabric on one of the tree branches. It was blue and gold, and a spark of familiarity crossed her mind.

"I've seen this before," she whispered. "This looks like—"

"Azra," Blade finished for her.

When Aura turned to where Blade was still pressed against the snowy ground, she found the former queen standing tall above him. The royal garments she had kept so neatly ironed were now ripped and torn, her hair was a tangled mess, and there were so many scars and bruises on her body that she looked like she'd just fought off an entire army of tigers. Aura almost felt sorry for her. She didn't look like the powerful witch she had briefly come to know. Now, she looked like a decrepit old woman, a helpless old woman who's desperate to regain some control over her life.

"It's you!" Blade exclaimed. "You killed him. You killed my father!"

Azra smirked, pulling the knife from behind her back that was still dripping with blood. She laughed. "No, my sweet boy. I merely immobilized him. The animals took care of the rest. Made my job that much easier. But maybe for my next kill, I'll make it a little more... personal."

Blade gasped as Azra grabbed him by the neck and lifted him off the ground. He gagged for air, his legs flailing, and his fingers attempting to wrestle himself free.

"Blade!" Aura shouted, catching Azra's attention.

"And you! If it weren't for you and your damn mother standing in my way, I wouldn't be like this. I should've killed all you abnormals when I had the chance!"

Aura took a step toward them, her fists clenched and her heart beating fast.

"Not so fast, foolish child," Azra warned. "Don't even think about taking another step... unless you want to start picking up pieces of your little boyfriend."

"Let him go, Azra," she demanded instead. "This isn't your fight. You won't win!" She turned to look at Blade. "Remember what you're capable of now," she said to him.

At that, Blade channeled his strength and cinched his teeth down into Azra's arm, hoping to penetrate her enough for her to free him before he mauls the rest of her. However, when he did, he only managed to inflict a minor pinch, his blunt teeth barely cutting through her thick skin.

Horrified, he glanced back at Aura, confused as to why he was still human. "I don't understand. I thought you turned me! Why isn't it working?"

Azra gripped her hand tighter now, cutting off his circulation, and Blade's face turned into a shade of light purple. "Aw, did your little girlfriend try turning you into a little vampire... and miserably failed?!" She looked over at Aura and then back at Blade. "At least one of you is dying tonight."

"Not if I can help it." A voice appeared out of nowhere, and blood spewed out of Azra's mouth, causing her to release Blade. When she eventually fell over, Marietta was standing there, the sharp blade she was holding still pierced inside the queen.

"Mother!" Aura ran over to hug her. "You saved us! But how did you know?"

Marietta smiled. "When you two never came home for supper, I knew something was wrong. I could sense it." She looked over at the rotting body of her husband. "And Cross, I suspected something had happened to him, but I didn't want to believe it." She wiped her tears with the back of her hand and sat beside the body. "If only I had protected him. If only I had turned him, he wouldn't be gone. I love you, Cross, and I'll never stop."

Aura only shook her head. "But Mother, I tried turning Blade. It doesn't work. I don't think it's possible."

Marietta sighed. "I should've told you earlier, but I didn't think you were going to try. You're not powerful enough to turn someone on your own because you're more human than you are vampire. Same with me. Not from a single bite, anyway. In order for a mortal to truly transform, you would need to die for him. Not only would you need to sacrifice your powers, but you'd also need to sacrifice your life."

"You mean..."

"Yes, the only way I could've saved Cross was if I sacrificed myself for him, died for him, something I now regret not doing." She reached out a hand and touched her husband's cheek. "He saved me, us. It's the least I could've done."

"No, it can't be, Mother. There has to be another way! I can't risk letting Blade die. I have to protect him. Tell me there's another way!"

"There is. You may not like the outcome, but there's a way to turn Blade and keep him safe. I've realized for quite some time now that it's becoming harder and harder for me to stay alert. My senses aren't what they used to be; if they were, Cross would still be alive. I've failed him, just like I've failed my mother and father. Just like I almost had you killed because I was so afraid of Azra ruining my life even more. And now, with the love of my life also gone, I don't think I have what it takes anymore to protect us and this town. The deaths are growing more and more each day, and this town needs someone who can actually help you save it."

"What are you trying to say?" Part of Aura knew where Marietta was headed, though she didn't want to admit it. She was scared, and she knew she had to choose between her mother and Blade.

"I think you already know, Aura." She stood up from where she sat and wrapped her arms around her daughter. "The only way for Blade to turn is if I sacrifice myself and give him my powers."

"No," Aura refused. "I won't let you. We can figure out a way to turn Blade without you having to die."

But Marietta only shook her head. "I'm afraid there is no other way. Even with Azra gone, there will always be someone, something, wreaking havoc on this town. Even as we speak, the Hibernians are seeking revenge on the royal family. If Blade doesn't turn, I'm afraid he won't have much time left."

"Mother, I can't. I can't lose you!" She held on tighter to Marietta, her tears staining her coat, and her words jumbling as she turned into a slobbering mess.

"It's okay. I'll only be doing myself a favor by doing this. I want to reunite with my love, Cross. And with him gone, I no longer see a reason to continue living. Everyone wins."

Blade seemed thrilled at the prospect of Marietta's proposal, but Aura, being the stubborn daughter that she was, stormed off. "Yeah, everyone wins... except for me!"

WITHOUT HER DAUGHTER'S APPROVAL, MARIETTA knew she couldn't transfer her vampirism to Blade. She couldn't leave Earth while on bad terms with Aura; it would only devastate the both of them. But she also missed Cross, dearly. She missed the way he used to wake her up every morning with a fresh cup of coffee in his hands, how he used to smile at her every night and tell her how happy he was to be with her.

As the days continued to go by without him in her life, her vitality grew significantly weaker. She had lost the motivation to continue pushing on, the devastation from the loss draining her of her essence. She'd stopped watching over the town and stopping criminals with Aura, and she'd even stopped drinking from the jars of human blood Aura would bring back.

"Mother," Aura said when she came into her room one morning.

Marietta was too weak to get out of bed. Her skin had turned more pale than usual, and she was losing more and more weight by the second. It was as if her body had reverted back to what it was when she feared the queen.

"Mother," Aura said again. "I can't bear to see you like this. What can I do to help? You need to drink. You need to get better."

"You can give me your blessing. Let me go, so I can reunite with my husband."

She shook her head. "I can't. I can't lose you. I've lost everyone I've ever loved. I can't lose you, too!"

"You have Blade. He can take care of you when I'm gone. He loves you. I see the way he looks at you. It's the same way Cross used to look at me. Trust me, Aura. You'd be more devastated with him gone. Besides, I've seen how you look when you come back in the mornings, bruised and beat up. Blade can help you protect the town, more than I'll ever can. Please, Aura, I'm suffering from this grief. Please let me go."

When Aura finally agreed and nodded her head, Marietta called in Blade, who could feel the tension in the room and decided to remain silent. She gestured him closer to her, and when he did, she slowly sunk her teeth into him and released her soul, transferring the spirit of her body into his. She felt her body growing frailer as Blade accepted the energy from her. Aura looked away. From what Marietta could guess, Aura didn't want to see the last moments of her mother's life, and she didn't blame her. And when the last drop finally left her body, she collapsed.

Marietta looked from where she was above the small town of Marsonia. It had become quieter than it used to be. The people were much calmer, and criminals were usually dealt with in a timely manner. The fate of the town she used to love was now in the hands of its new guardians, Aura and Blade, who hid in the darkness and only came out when the people needed protecting. She watched in pride and contentment as they drained those who deserved to be drained and saved those who deserved to be saved.

"How are our kids doing?" Cross asked as he wrapped his arms around her and rested his chin on her shoulder.

Life in the sky was much different than how she envisioned it would be. She always feared death, afraid of the unknown and the potential for eternal misery. But it was nothing like what she'd seen in her nightmares. Her limbs weren't being torn apart, and fire wasn't reigning down on her. The stress and anxiety she experienced back down on Earth had completely vanished, and she almost forgot why she had even let herself suffer in the first place.

She looked over to her right. Her mother and father were dancing on the clouds, her head resting on his shoulder, and his hand resting on her waist. She looked over to her left, where Blackwell and Azra reunited as a family, along with Nicolo. Everyone seemed so different from how they were back down on Earth. Life felt lighter up here, more peaceful, just like how Marsonia used to be.

"They're getting there, not perfect, but I'm hopeful."

Aura sunk her teeth down hard onto a man's left shoulder, bringing back memories of when she used to drink for play and survival. The familiarity of digging her fangs into men who tried to abuse her brought her a sense of satisfaction. She felt powerful, like she was in control.

But this time, she didn't drink out of boredom or to relieve the anxieties she had about her mother. This time, she drank for revenge, revenge for herself and revenge for all the innocent people who had been killed ever since the two halves merged. And it wasn't only the Lucerians who turned to the side of evil, resorting to murder instead of sharing the wealth they had with the lower class. The Hibernians, once good citizens of Marsonia, also turned dark. They saw the upper-class as people who invaded their land, stealing their resources, and taking their people. And after what Queen Azra had done, the Hibernians could never quite get over the grudge.

"Hey, Aura," Blade shouted over. "Can I get a little help?"

She looked over at Blade, his beautiful eyes glistening in the moonlight, and realized that he was up against four drug dealers while she'd been busy snacking on the limp body in her hands. Their relationship never returned to how it used to be before they found out that they shared the same father. But still, they found themselves catching feelings for each other every now and then, accepting their fate as what it was instead of fighting it with their morality.

She dropped the body and rushed over, taking down half the men while Blade took care of the rest. He was still new to this; his strength and skills nowhere near as refined as Aura's, but he was getting a hang of it. Her mother's essence had fused in with his nicely, and his body had begun accepting it. And despite Aura's fear, Blade remained the same as he'd always been before the transformation, the same kind and compassionate Blade who helped out his sister when he wasn't out saving the town.

Blade finished draining the last of the crooks before kneeling down against the wall and catching his breath. "I don't know if I can keep doing this, Aura. There are too many of them. I'm struggling to keep up. I have no idea how you do it."

Aura perched beside him and took a deep breath. He had a point. Why are they even doing this? It's a job that will never be complete, even after they're dead. The crimes in Marsonia would never stop, not as long as people existed. And what about the rest of the world? The people they *aren't* trying to save? Sure, people looked up to them, saw them as heroes, but it's that same spirit that got Vladimir killed.

She stood up and walked toward the edge of the roof before looking down onto the bustling streets below. Nothing but screams and the sound of gunshots.

"Maybe," she finally responded. "Maybe this *is* just a waste of time. I always envisioned my life living on the coast of Italy, sipping some red wine, and staring off into the beautiful blue water the Mediterranean Sea had to offer. Perhaps, take a few art classes and make my way over to Paris. You know, travel, see the world, just like my mother always wanted." She sat back down beside Blade. "But when I stop to think about it more, I wonder. Is my life really about me? Or do I owe it to my family to carry on their wishes and defend those who can't defend themselves? After all, what good is being a vampire if I don't use my abilities for good? What good is being a vampire if I just run away and let all these people die? I know I can't save the world. It's impossible, but the least I can do is try. Save as many as I can before I die. And you should know that better than anyone, Blade. My mother gave up her life so you can live. The least you can do is return the favor."

"I know... but I just don't want my life with you to end. I don't want to risk losing you, Aura."

She kissed him on the cheek. "You won't. See those stars up there?" She pointed at the two brightest ones in the night sky. "Those are our parents, reunited, and happily in love, looking down on us and wishing us the same. If we ever do get separated, one day, we'll reunite and end up like them." She turned to him. "I love you, Blade, and I love that you've been by my side this entire time. And there's nothing I'd rather do than run off with you where no one can find us." She grabbed his hand and stood him up. Then the two of them walked back over to the edge again, staring out into the vast community of lights. "But the streets are my calling. It's my duty to protect the people. It's my duty to finish what my family started."

About the Author

Viola Tempest is a dystopian fantasy and paranormal romance author who yearns to expose the truth of those in the modern world: the good, the bad, and the ugly. Her inspiration primarily stems from life experiences, those who annoy her, ex-boyfriends, and the crazy dreams that pop into her head every once in a while.